DISNEY · PIXAR
INCREDIBLES 2

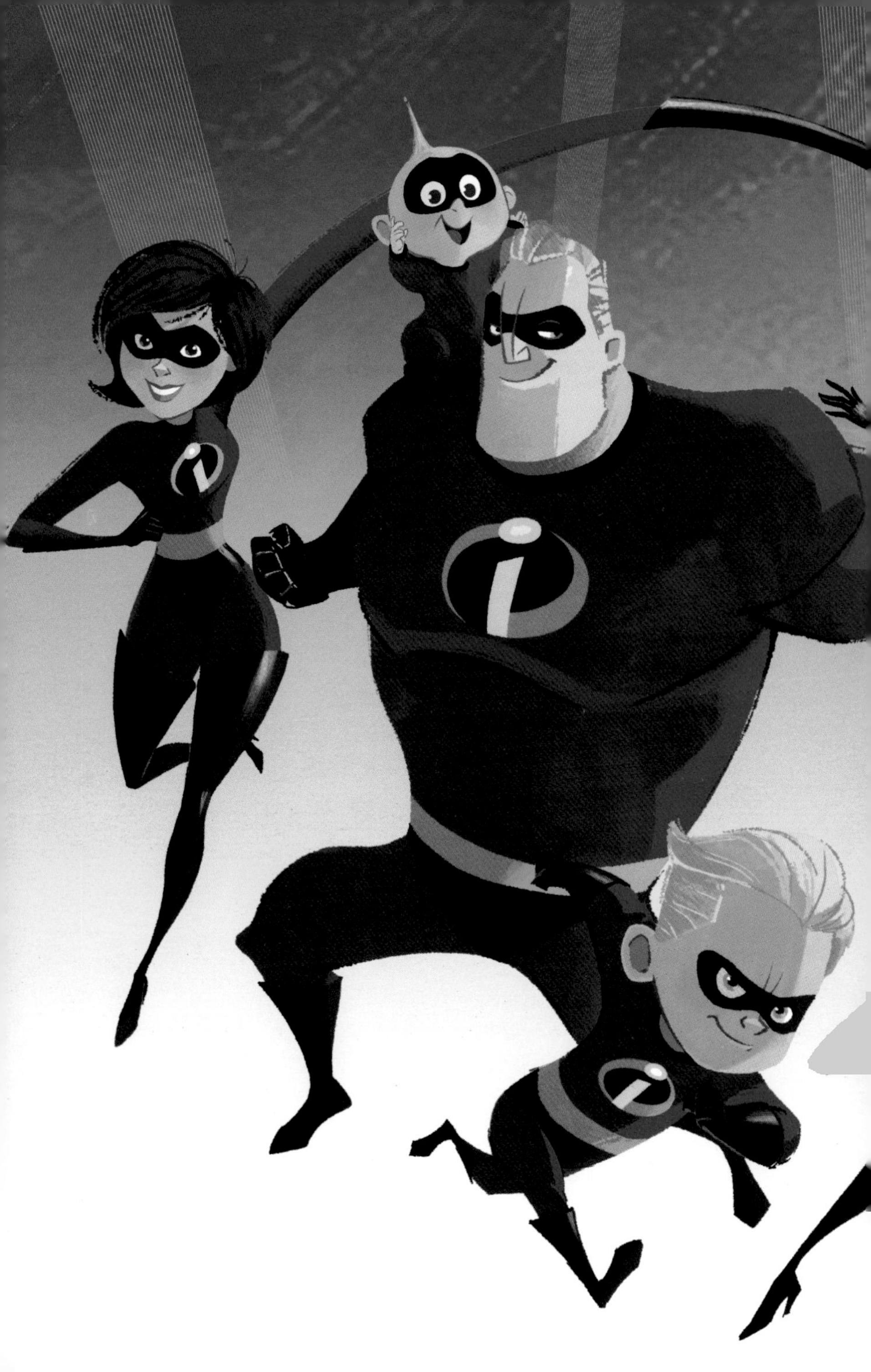

DISNEY · PIXAR
INCREDIBLES 2

Heroes at Home

Script by
Liz Marsham

Art by
Nicoletta Baldari

Lettering by
Chris Dickey

Dark Horse Books

Violet Parr

Violet is the oldest of the three Parr children. Fourteen years old, she is intelligent, sarcastic, and a little socially awkward—but she isn't afraid to speak her mind. Violet has two Super powers: she can become invisible and create force fields.

Dashiell "Dash" Parr

Dash is the middle child in the Parr family. Ten years old, he is adventurous, curious, competitive, and a little bit of a show-off. Dash has the power of super speed, and he doesn't want to hold back using it!

Jack-Jack Parr

Jack-Jack is a typical toddler—
at least as far as the rest of the Parr
family is aware. He talks baby-talk,
makes messes at mealtime, and gets into
things he shouldn't. But Jack-Jack actually
has an array of hidden Super powers.

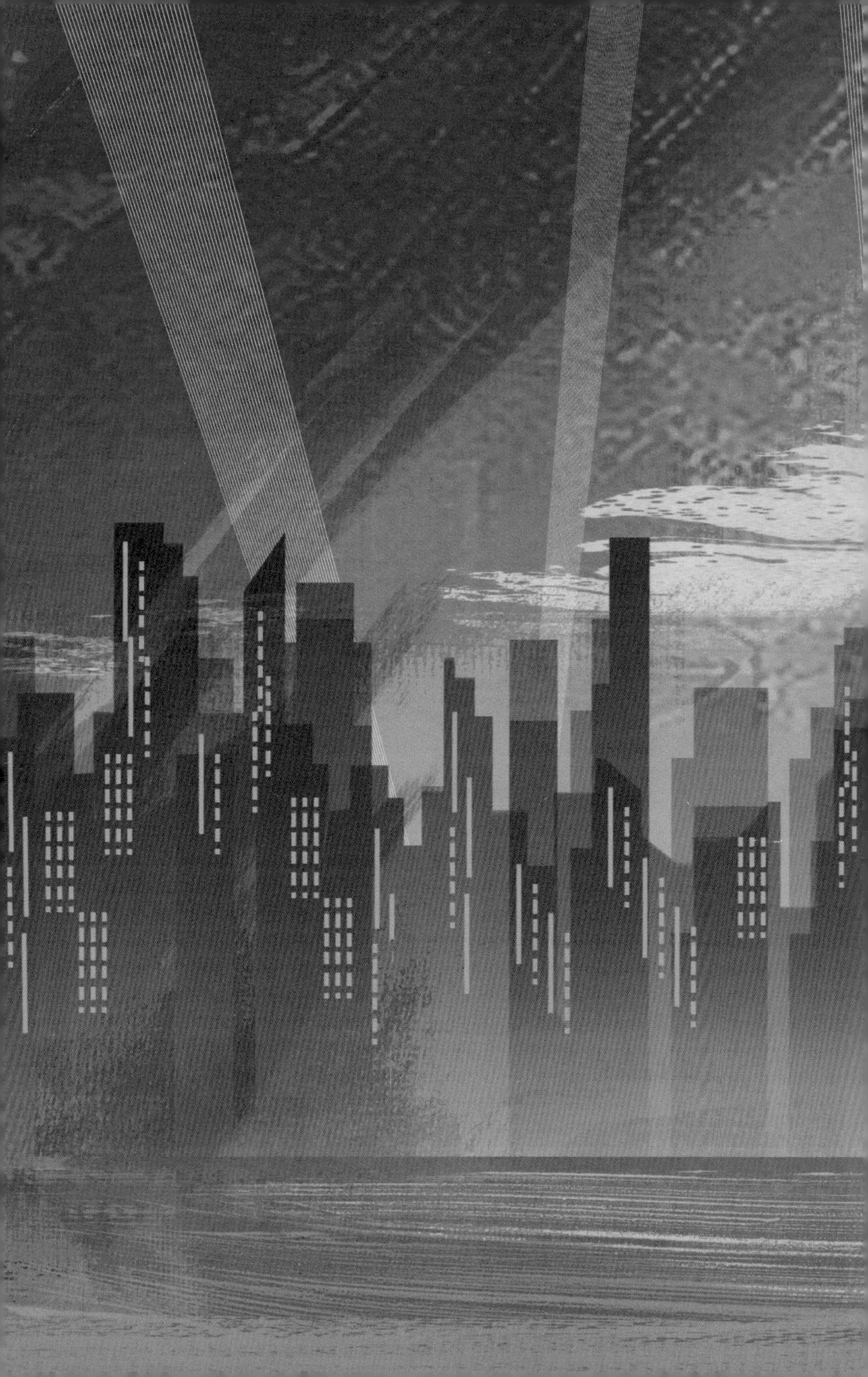

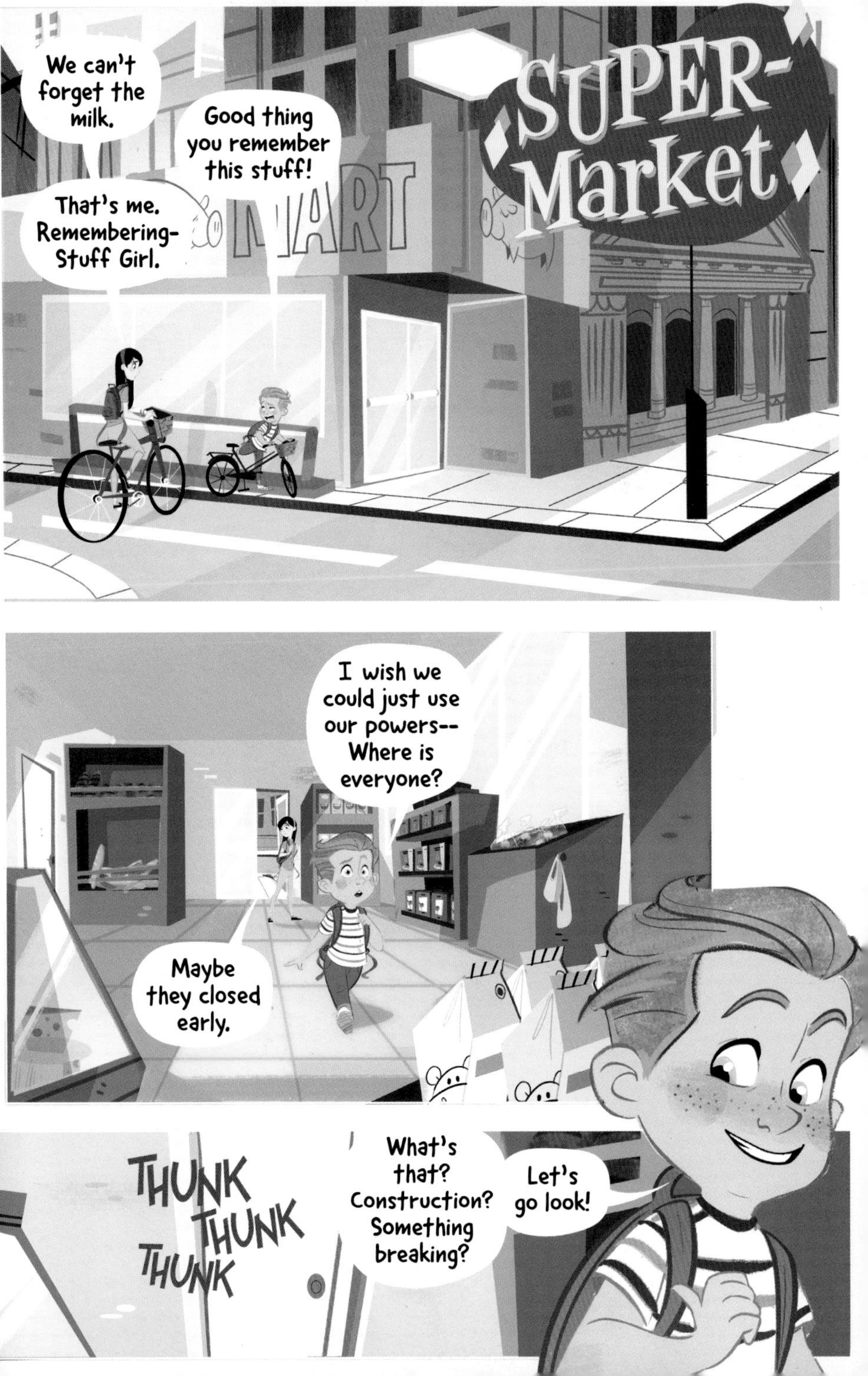

SUPER-Market
MART
We can't forget the milk.
Good thing you remember this stuff!
That's me. Remembering-Stuff Girl.
I wish we could just use our powers-- Where is everyone?
Maybe they closed early.
THUNK THUNK THUNK
What's that? Construction? Something breaking?
Let's go look!

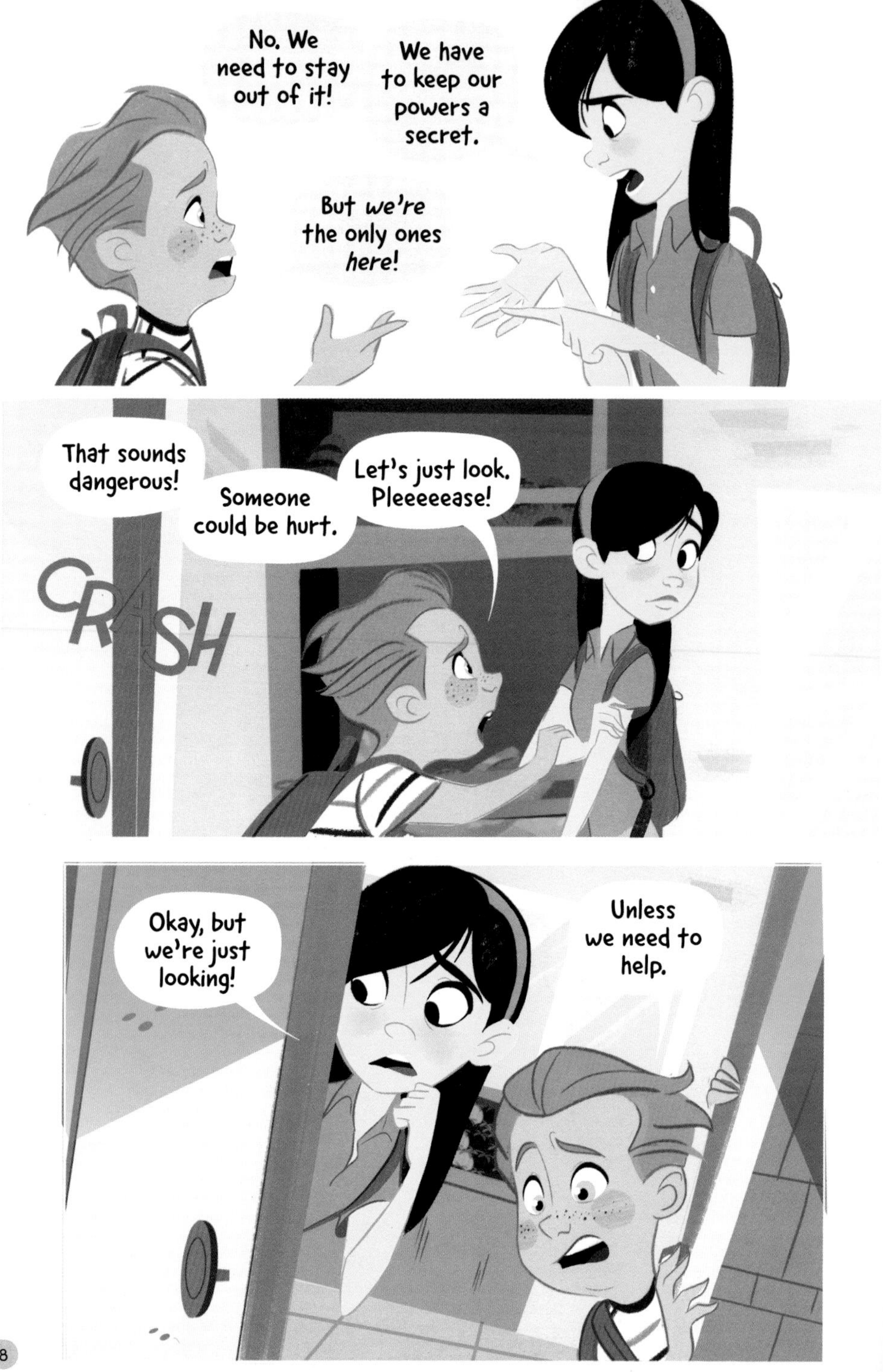
No. We need to stay out of it!
We have to keep our powers a secret.
But *we're* the only ones *here*!
That sounds dangerous!
Someone could be hurt.
Let's just look. Pleeeeease!
CRASH
Okay, but we're just looking!
Unless we need to help.

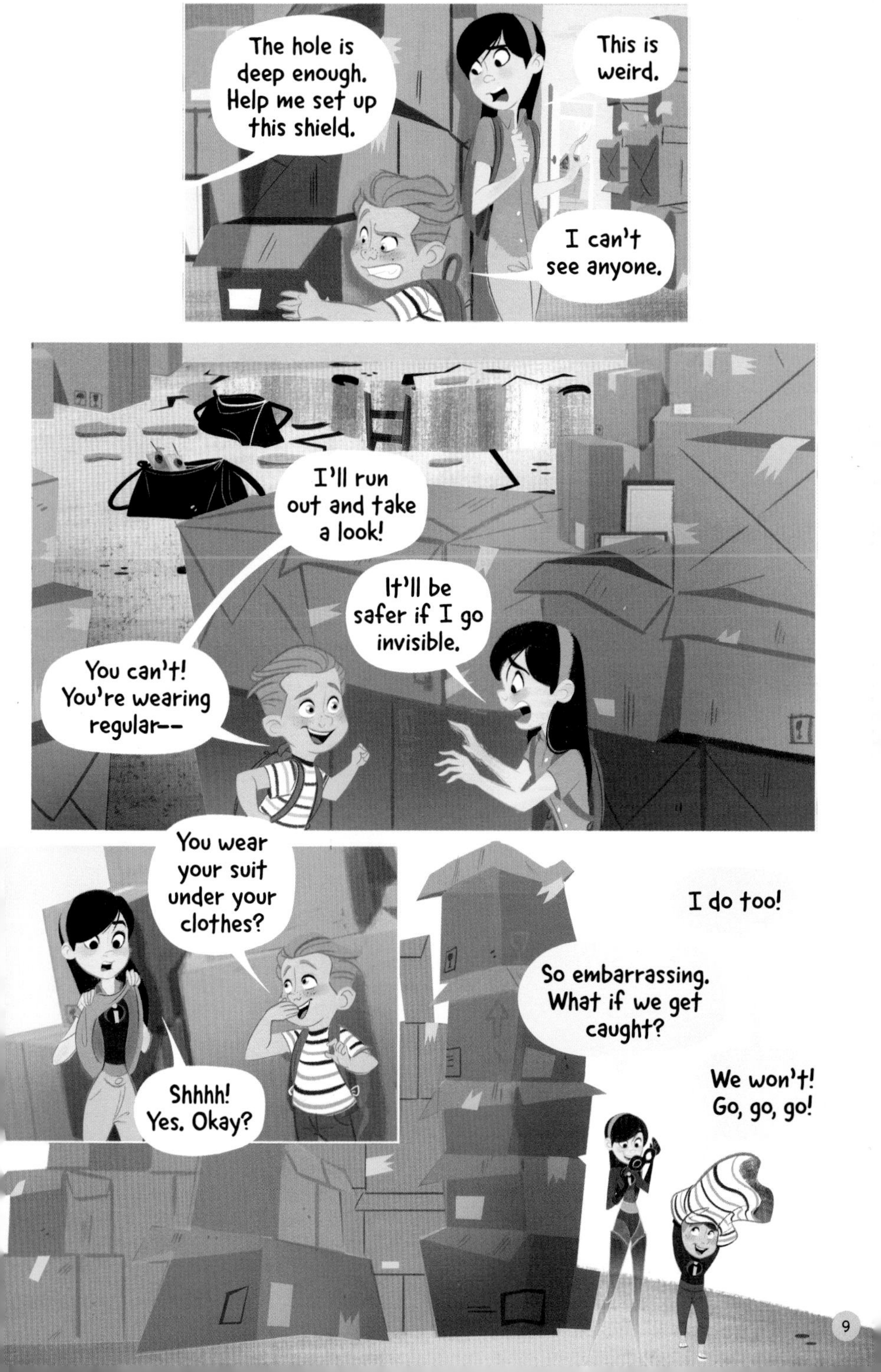
The hole is deep enough. Help me set up this shield.
This is weird.
I can't see anyone.
I'll run out and take a look!
It'll be safer if I go invisible.
You can't! You're wearing regular--
You wear your suit under your clothes?
Shhhh! Yes. Okay?
I do too!
So embarrassing. What if we get caught?
We won't! Go, go, go!

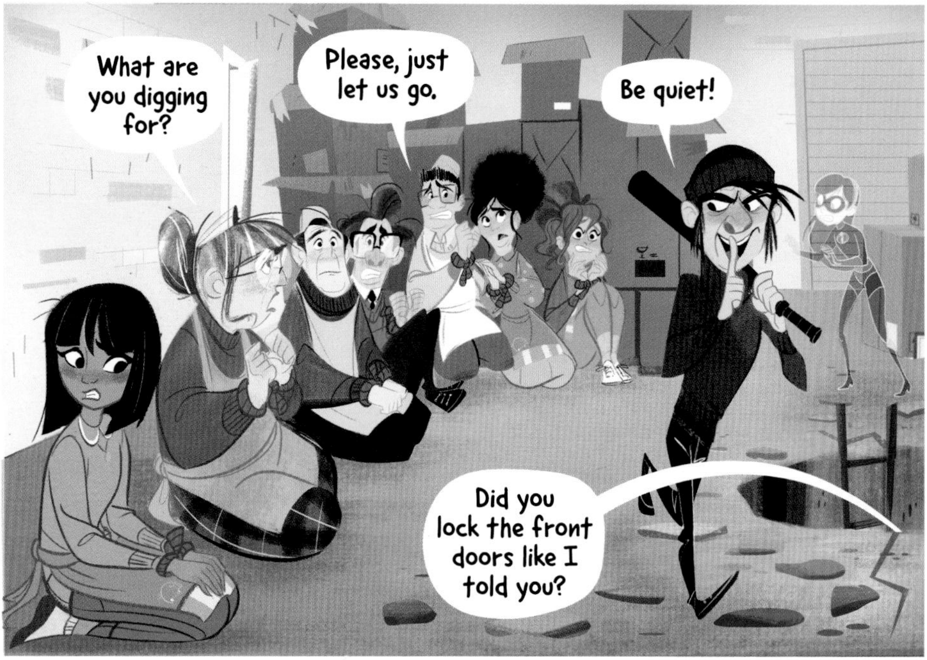
What are you digging for?
Please, just let us go.
Be quiet!
Did you lock the front doors like I told you?

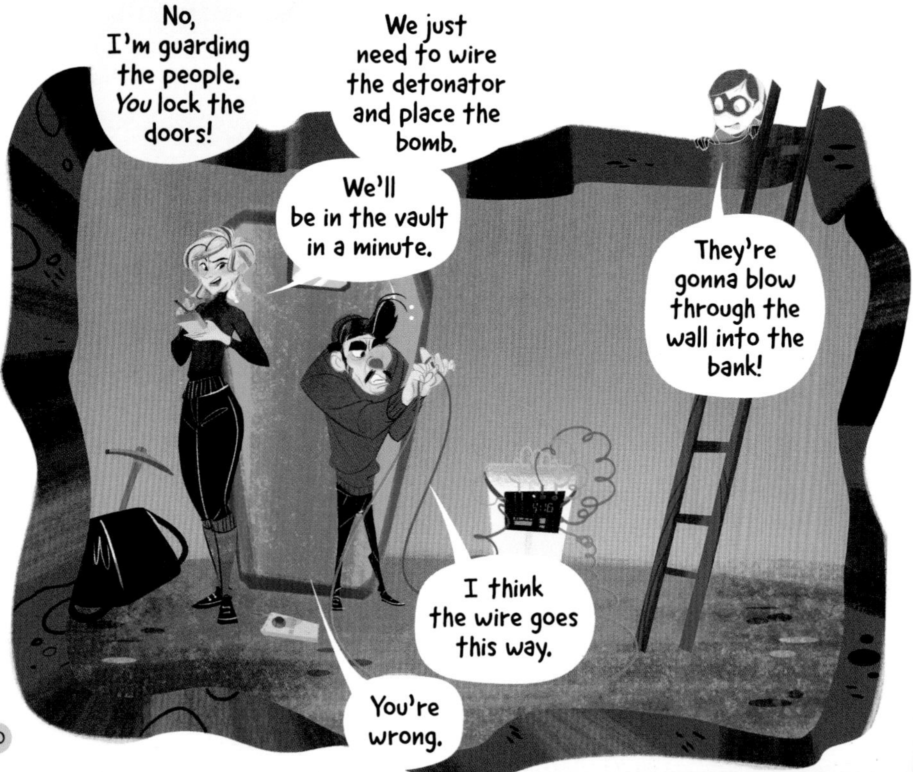
No, I'm guarding the people. *You* lock the doors!
We just need to wire the detonator and place the bomb.
We'll be in the vault in a minute.
They're gonna blow through the wall into the bank!
I think the wire goes this way.
You're wrong.

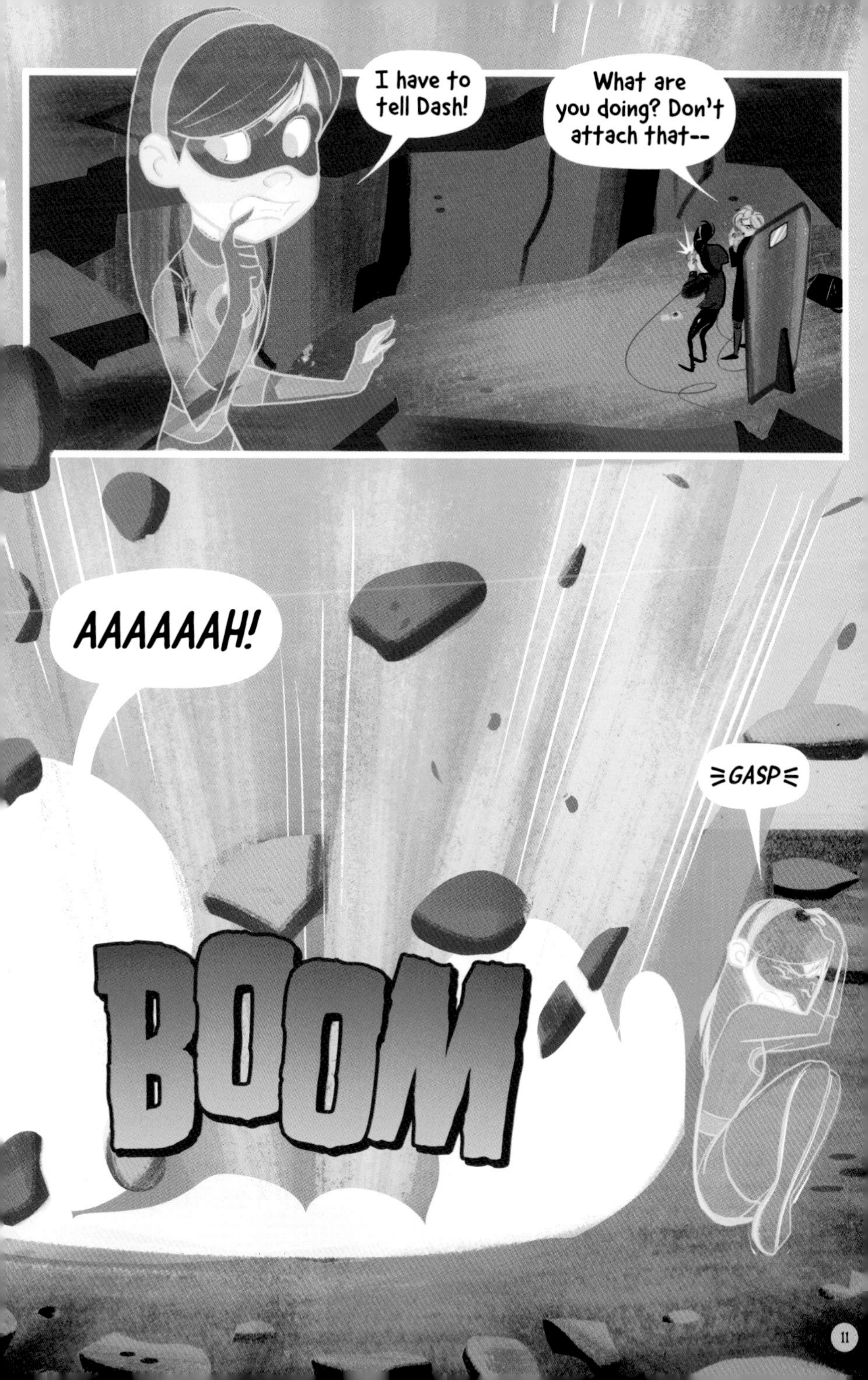
I have to tell Dash!
What are you doing? Don't attach that--
AAAAAAH!
GASP
BOOM

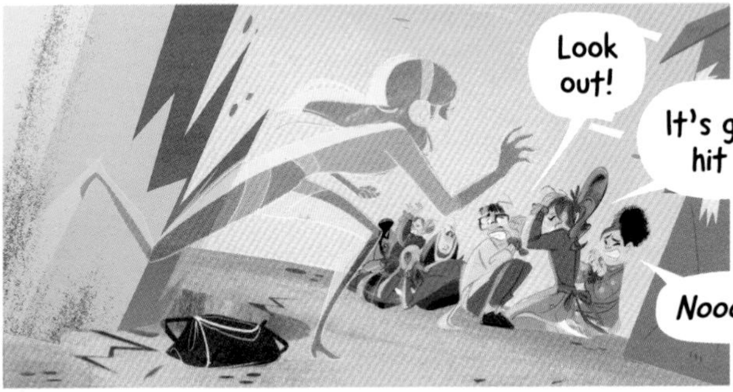
Look out!
It's gonna hit us!
Noooo!

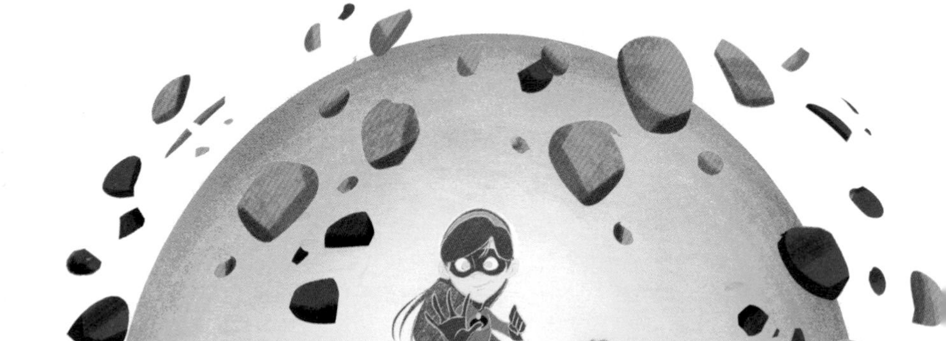
THUNK

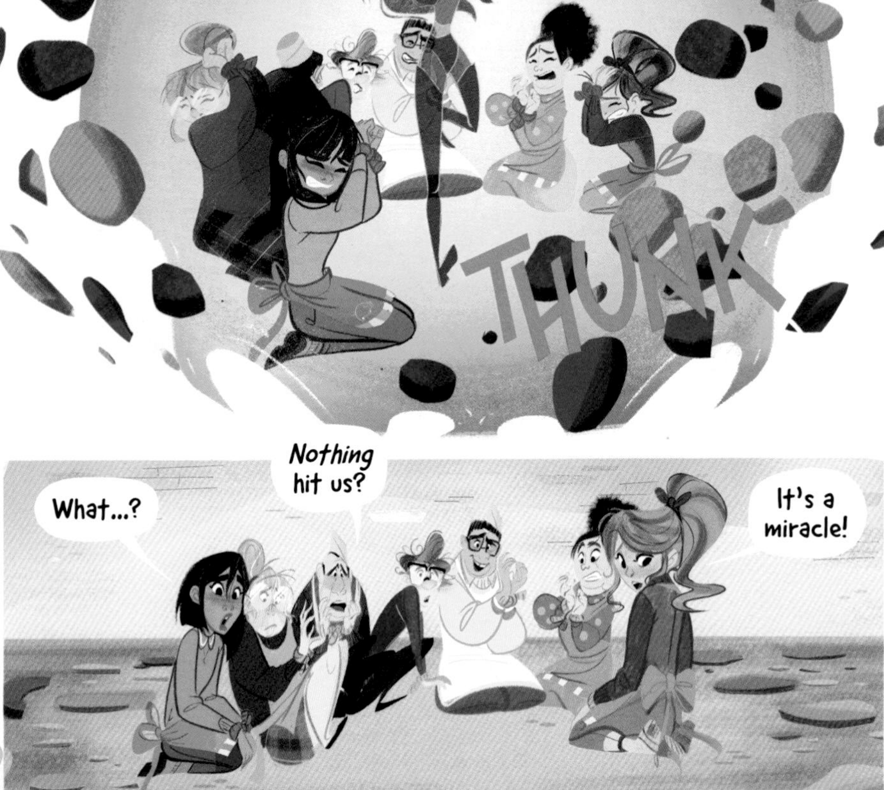
What...?
Nothing hit us?
It's a miracle!

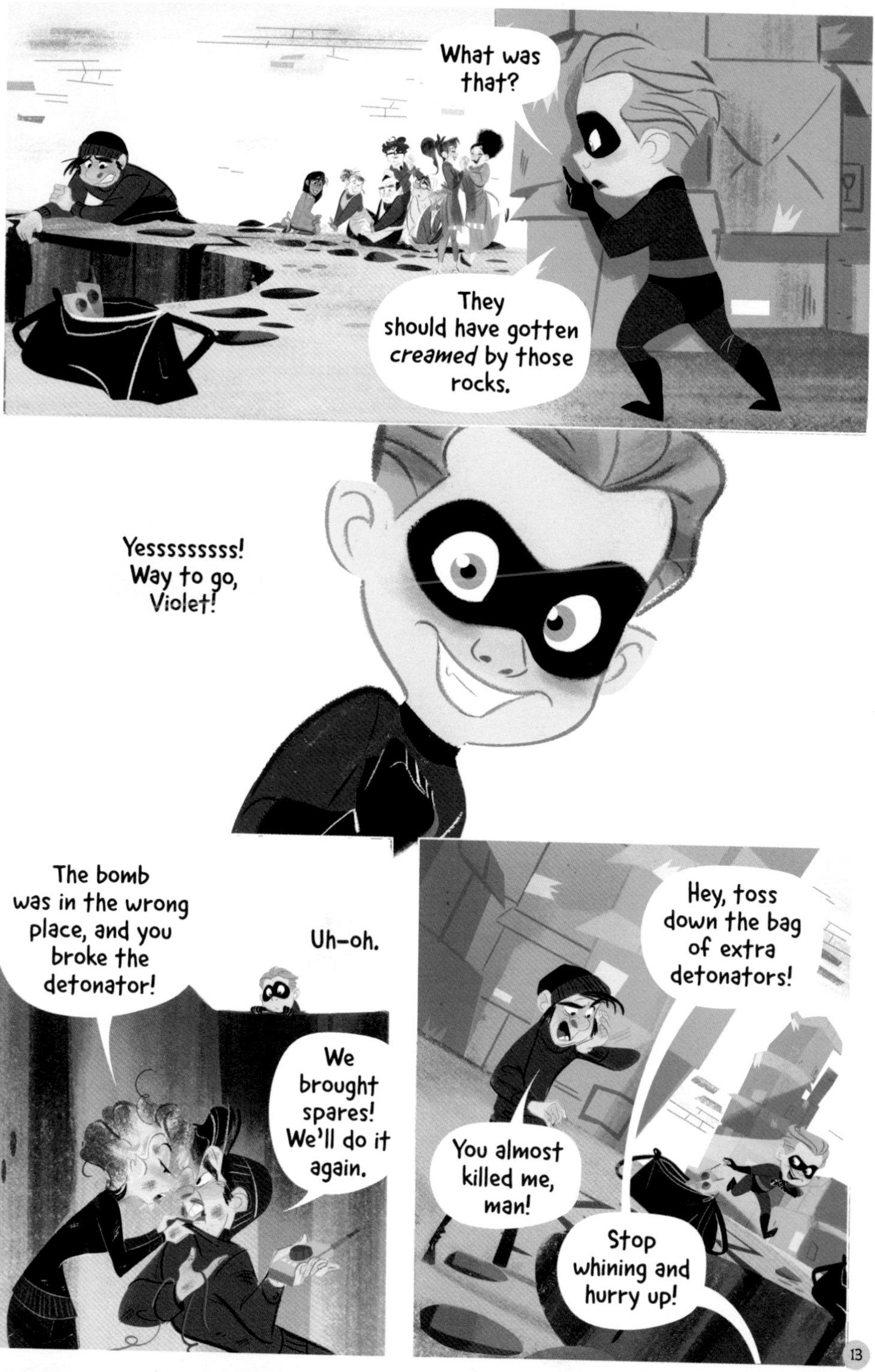
What was that?
They should have gotten *creamed* by those rocks.
Yesssssssss! Way to go, Violet!
The bomb was in the wrong place, and you broke the detonator!
Uh-oh.
We brought spares! We'll do it again.
Hey, toss down the bag of extra detonators!
You almost killed me, man!
Stop whining and hurry up!

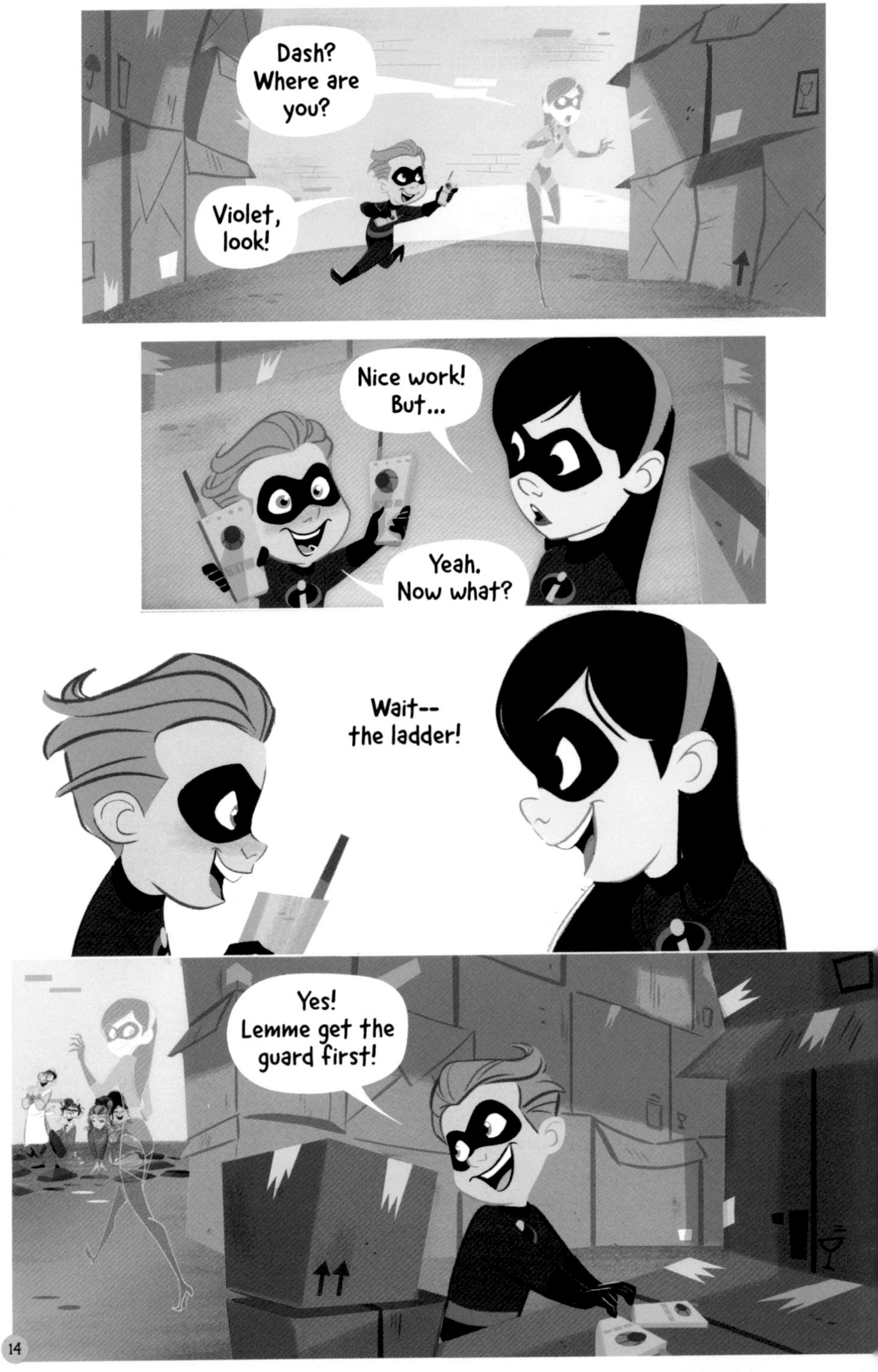
Dash? Where are you?
Violet, look!
Nice work! But...
Yeah. Now what?
Wait-- the ladder!
Yes! Lemme get the guard first!

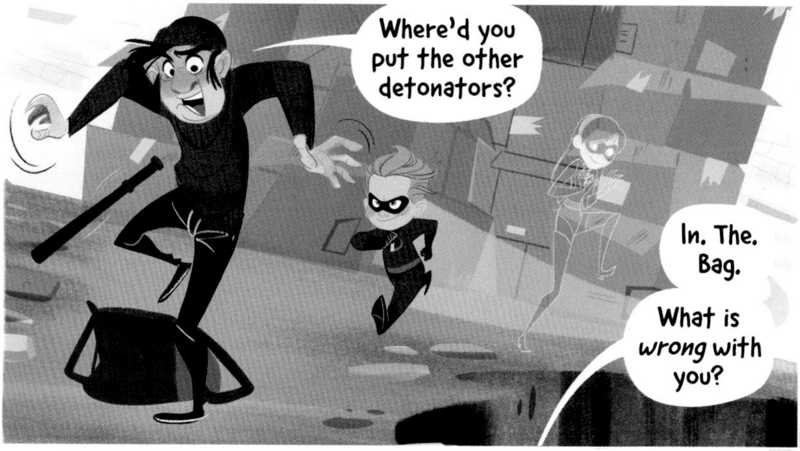
Where'd you put the other detonators?
In. The. Bag.
What is *wrong* with you?

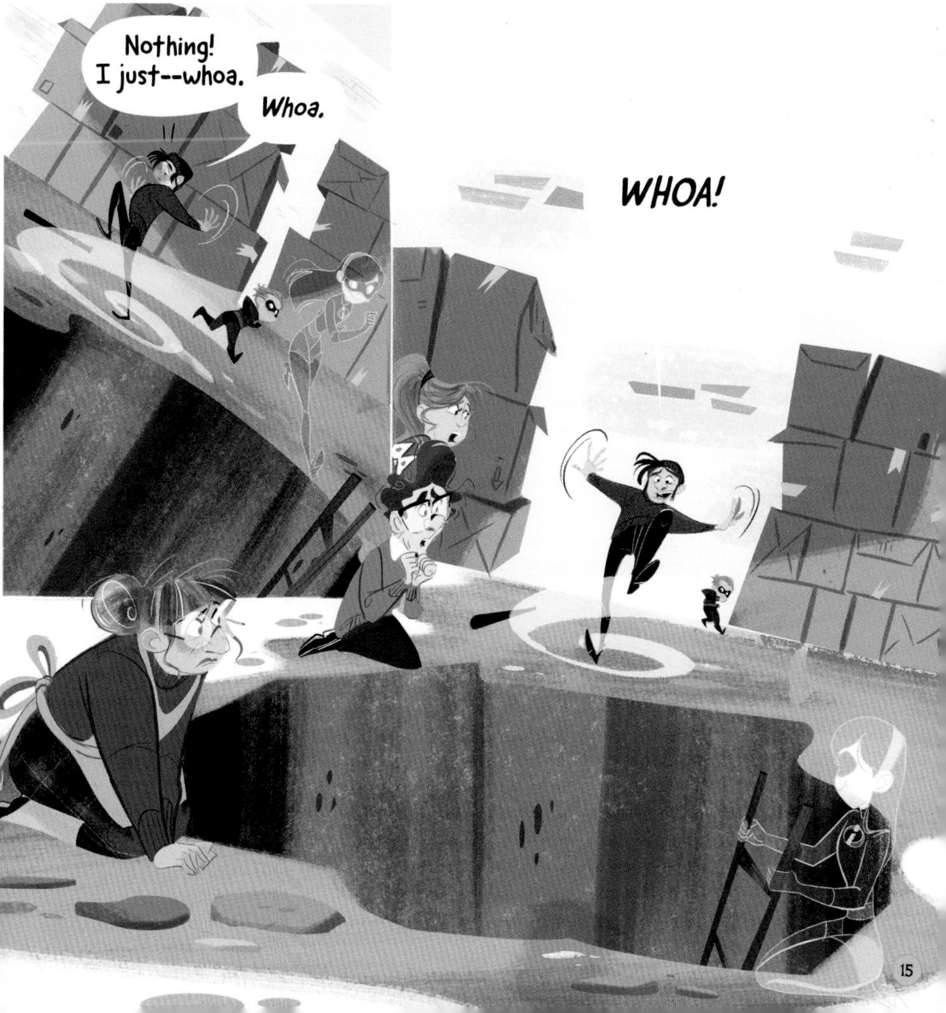
Nothing! I just--whoa.
Whoa.
WHOA!

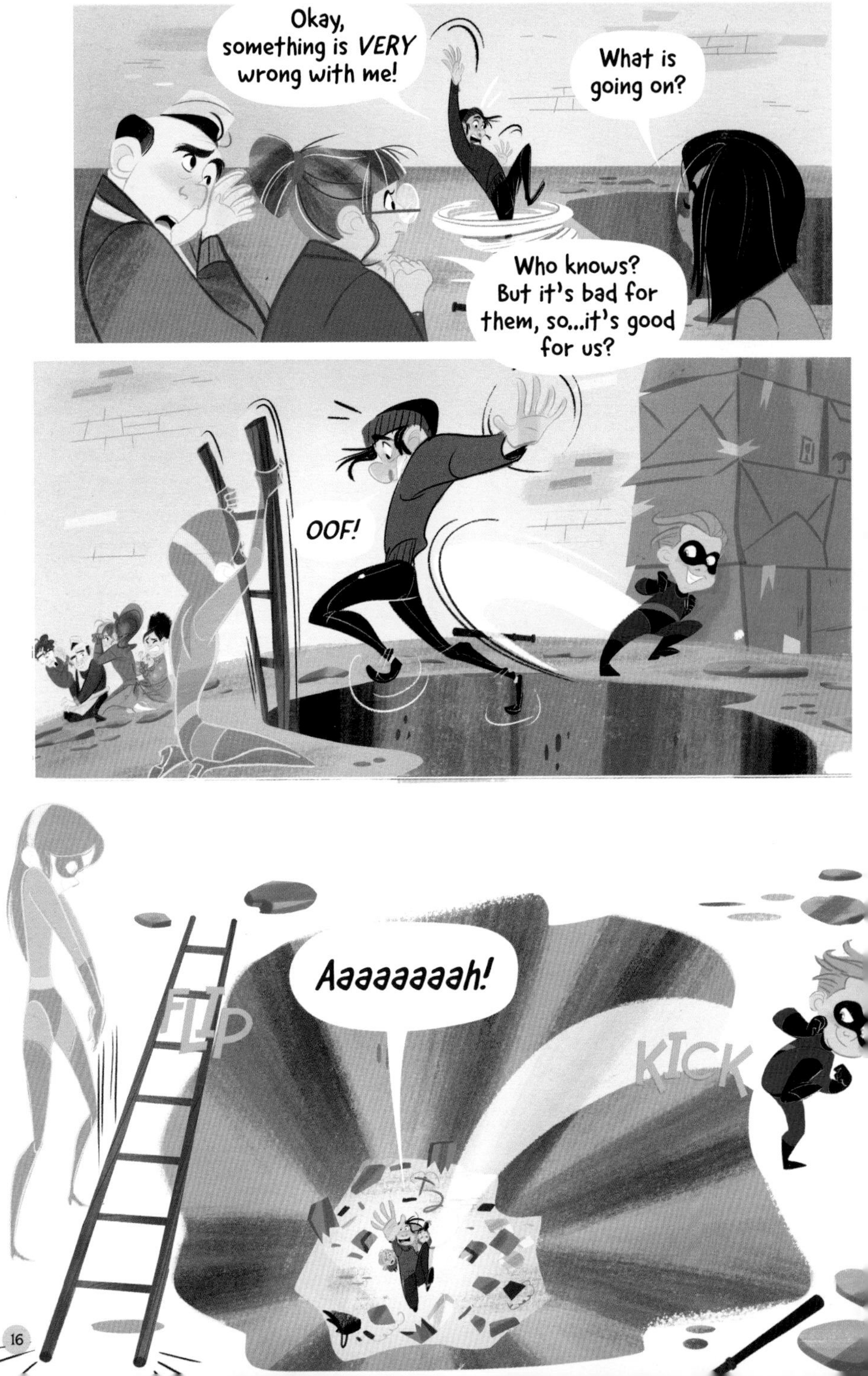
Okay, something is VERY wrong with me!
What is going on?
Who knows? But it's bad for them, so...it's good for us?
OOF!
Aaaaaaaah!
FLIP
KICK

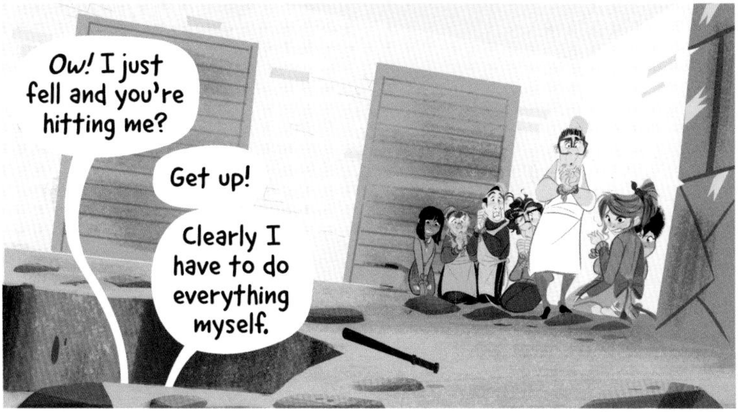

Ow! I just fell and you're hitting me?
Get up!
Clearly I have to do everything myself.

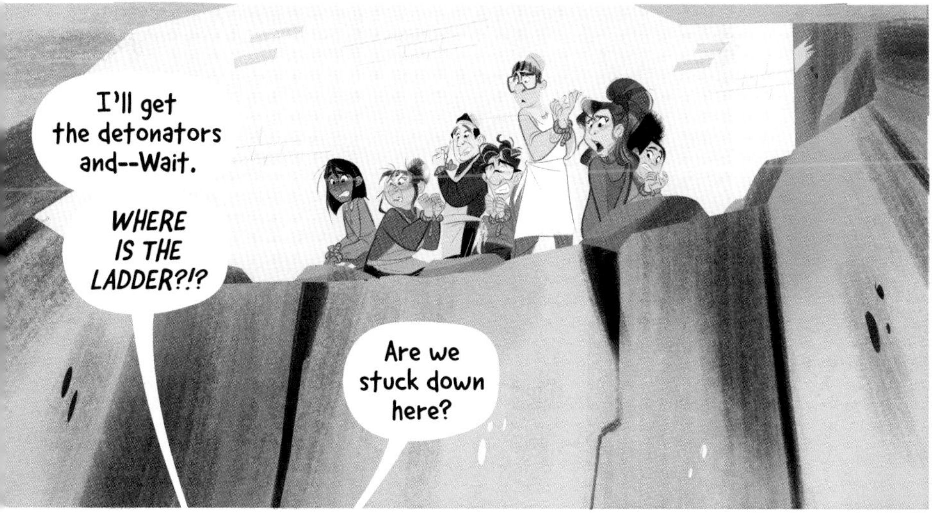

I'll get the detonators and--Wait.
WHERE IS THE LADDER?!?
Are we stuck down here?

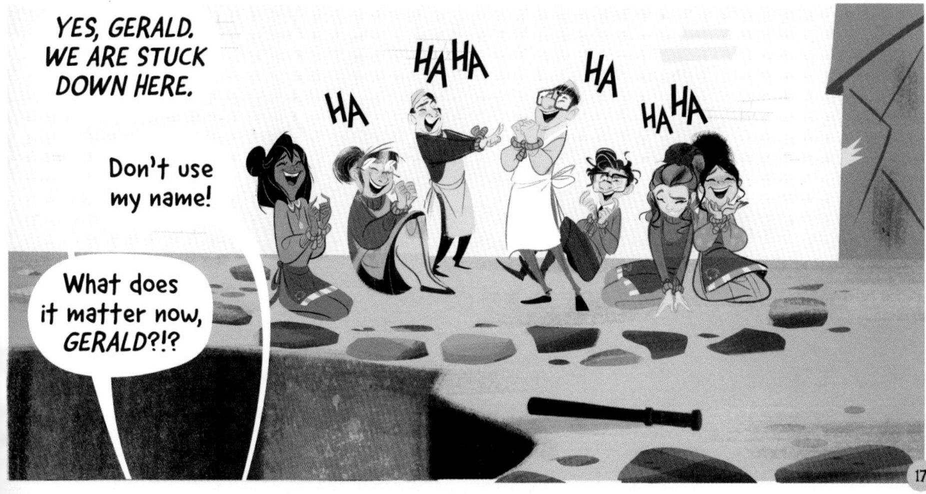

YES, GERALD. WE ARE STUCK DOWN HERE.
HA
HAHA
HA
HAHA
Don't use my name!
What does it matter now, *GERALD?!?*

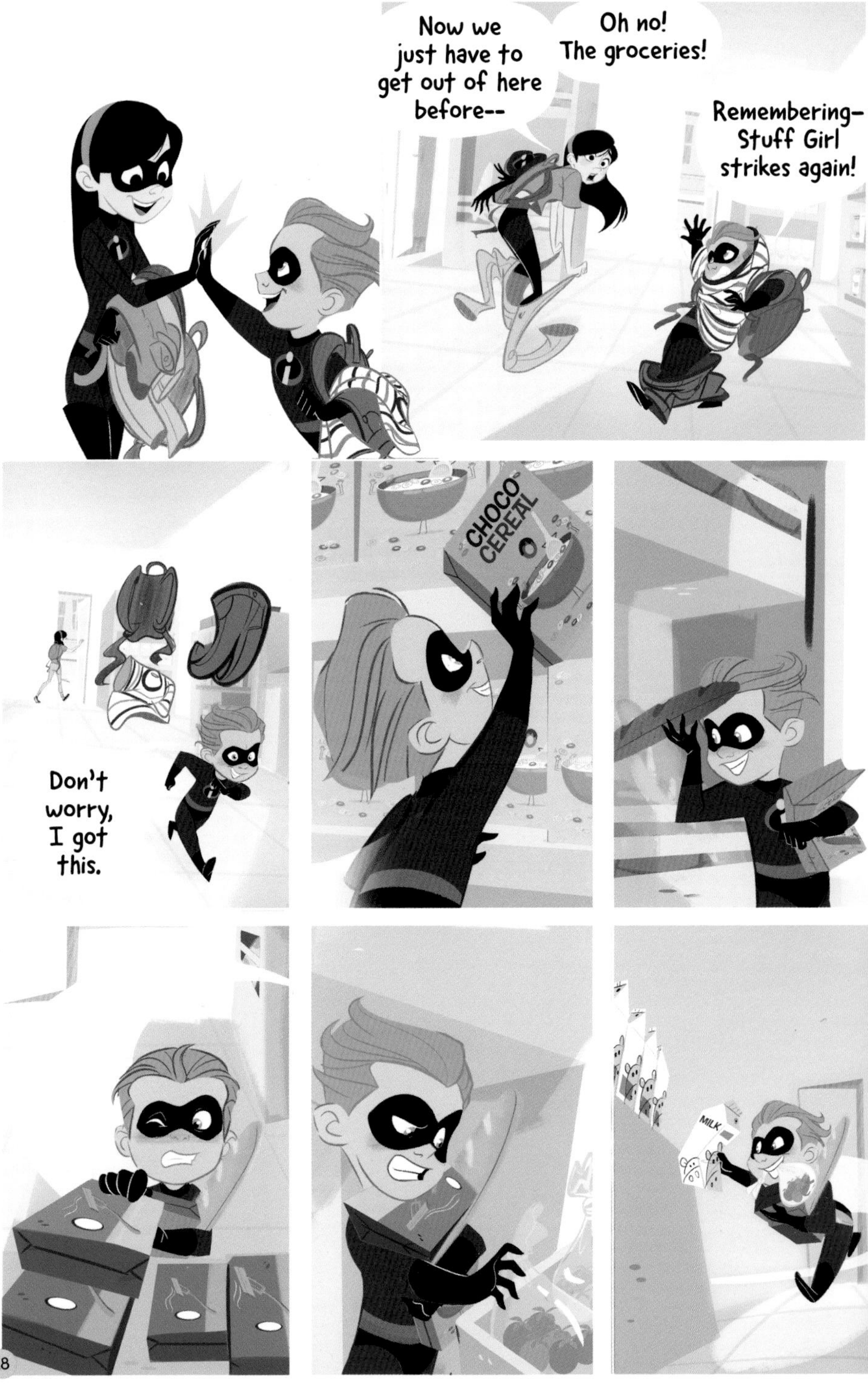

Now we just have to get out of here before--
Oh no! The groceries!
Remembering-Stuff Girl strikes again!
Don't worry, I got this.
CHOCO CEREAL
MILK

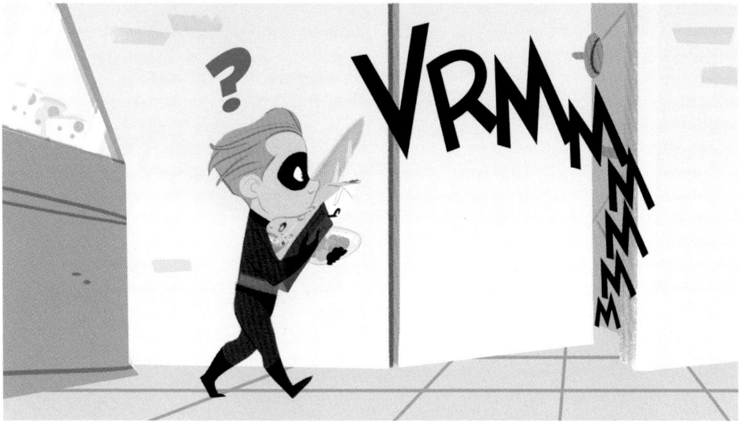
?
VRMMMMMM

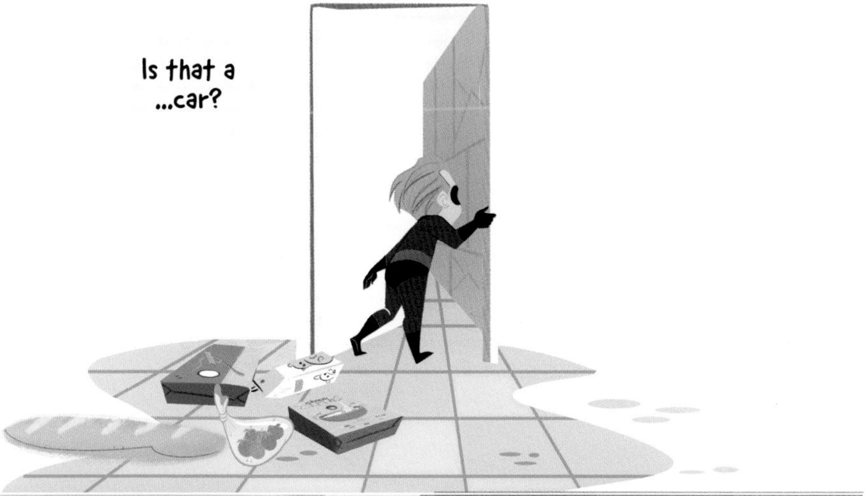
Is that a ...car?

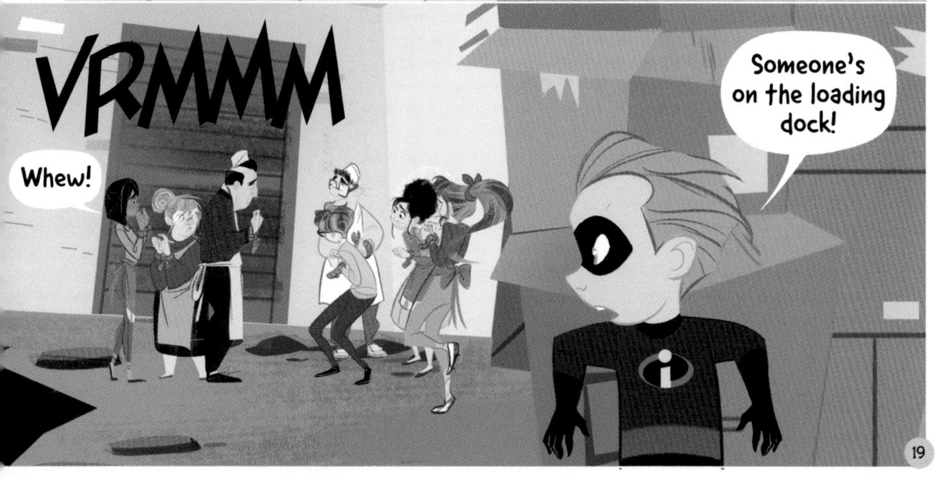
VRMMM
Whew!
Someone's on the loading dock!

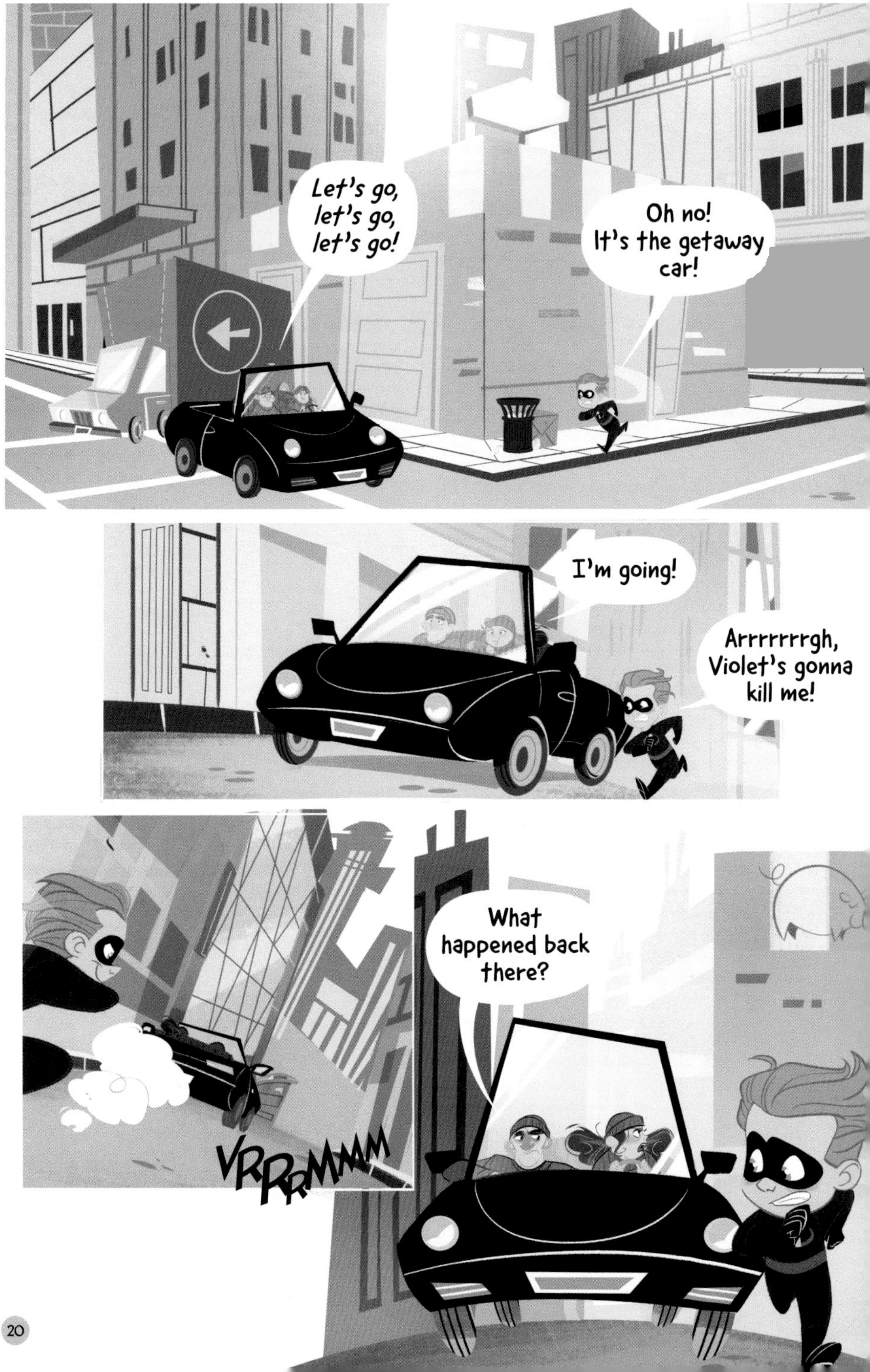
Let's go,
let's go,
let's go!
Oh no!
It's the getaway
car!
I'm going!
Arrrrrrrgh,
Violet's gonna
kill me!
VRRRMMM
What
happened back
there?

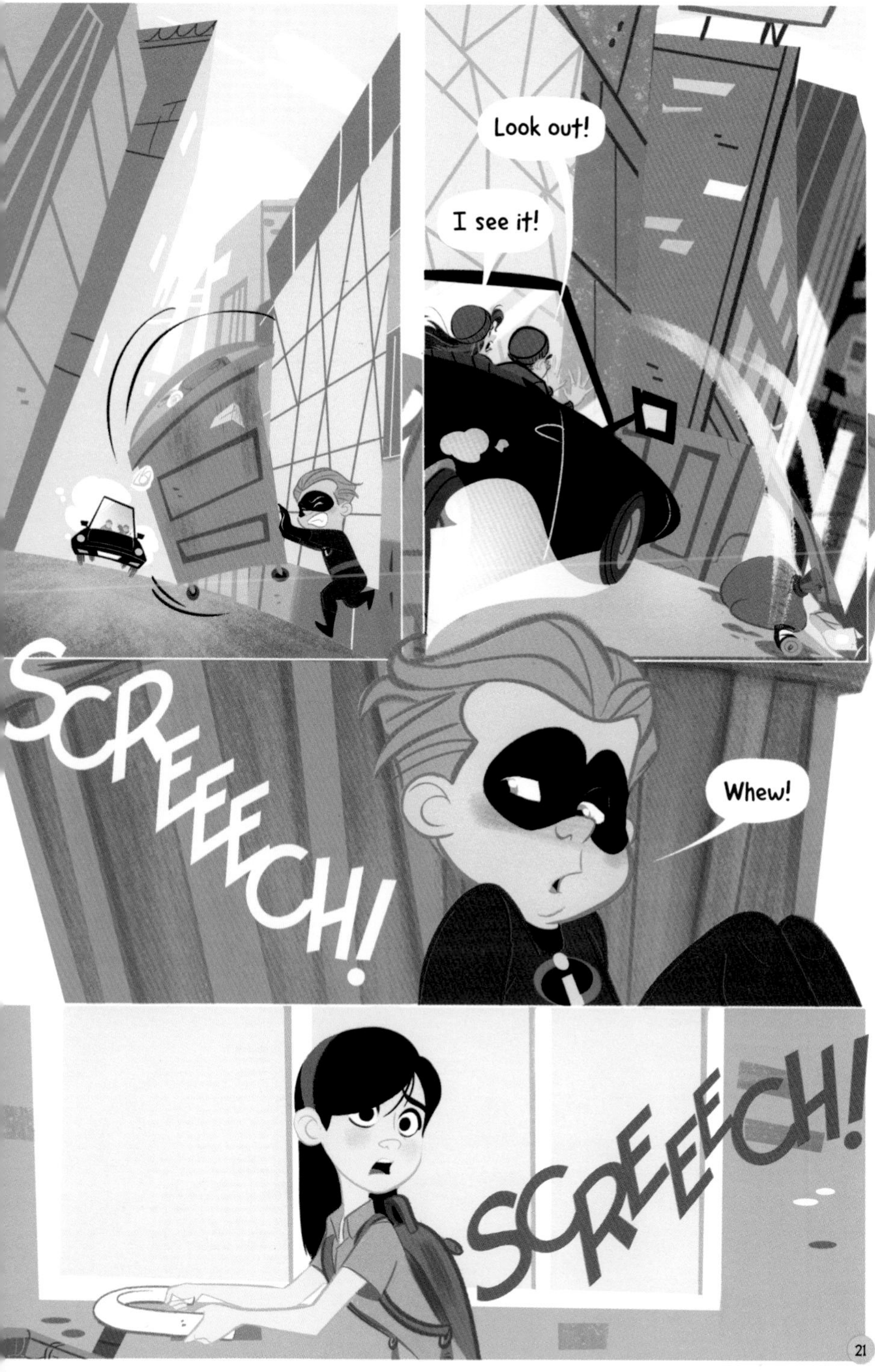
Look out!
I see it!
SCREEECH!
Whew!
SCREEECH!

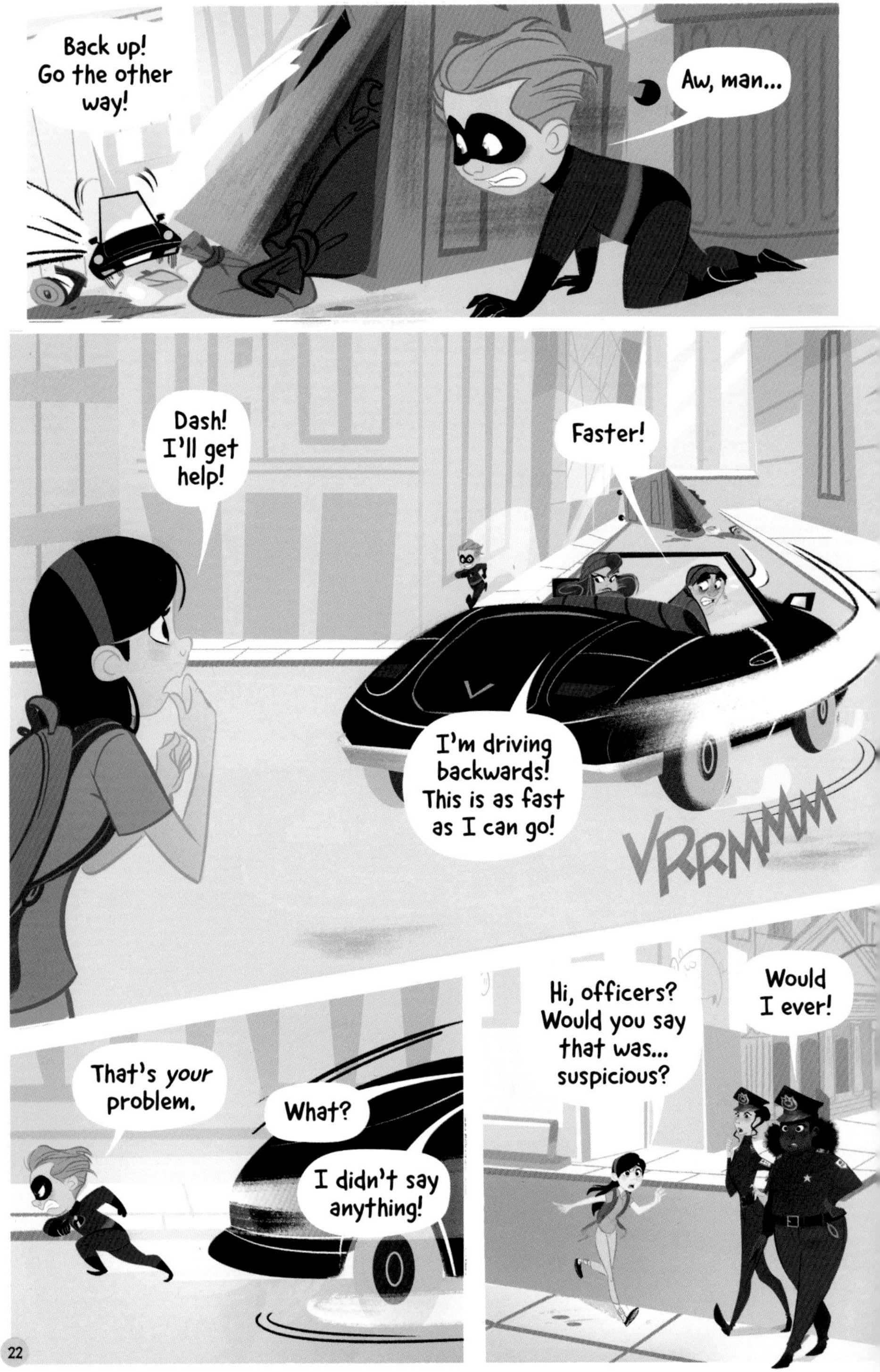
Back up! Go the other way!
Aw, man...
Dash! I'll get help!
Faster!
I'm driving backwards! This is as fast as I can go!
VRRMMM
That's *your* problem.
What?
I didn't say anything!
Hi, officers? Would you say that was... suspicious?
Would I ever!

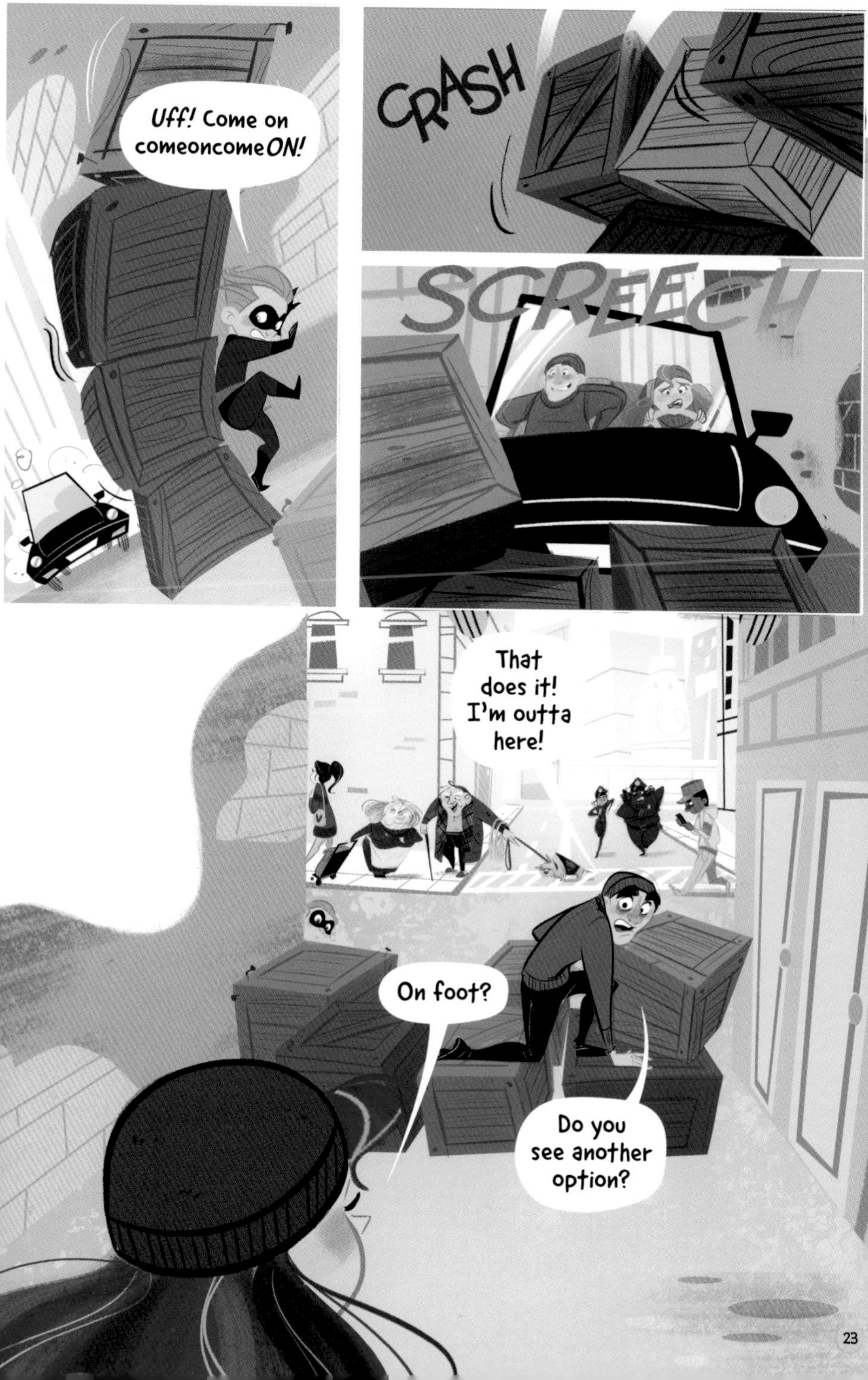
Uff! Come on comeoncomeON!
CRASH
SCREECH
That does it! I'm outta here!
On foot?
Do you see another option?

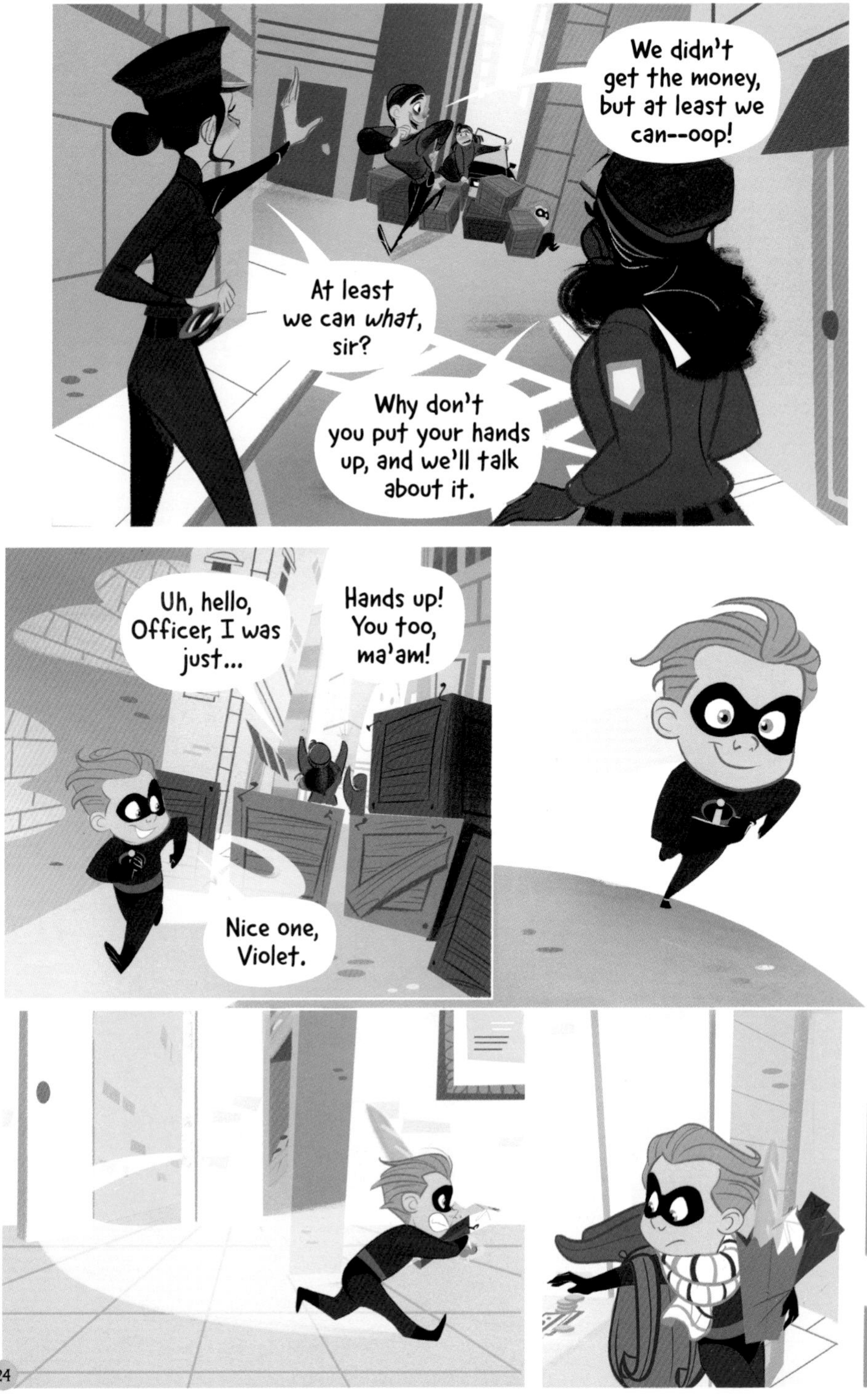
We didn't get the money, but at least we can--oop!
At least we can *what*, sir?
Why don't you put your hands up, and we'll talk about it.
Uh, hello, Officer, I was just...
Hands up! You too, ma'am!
Nice one, Violet.

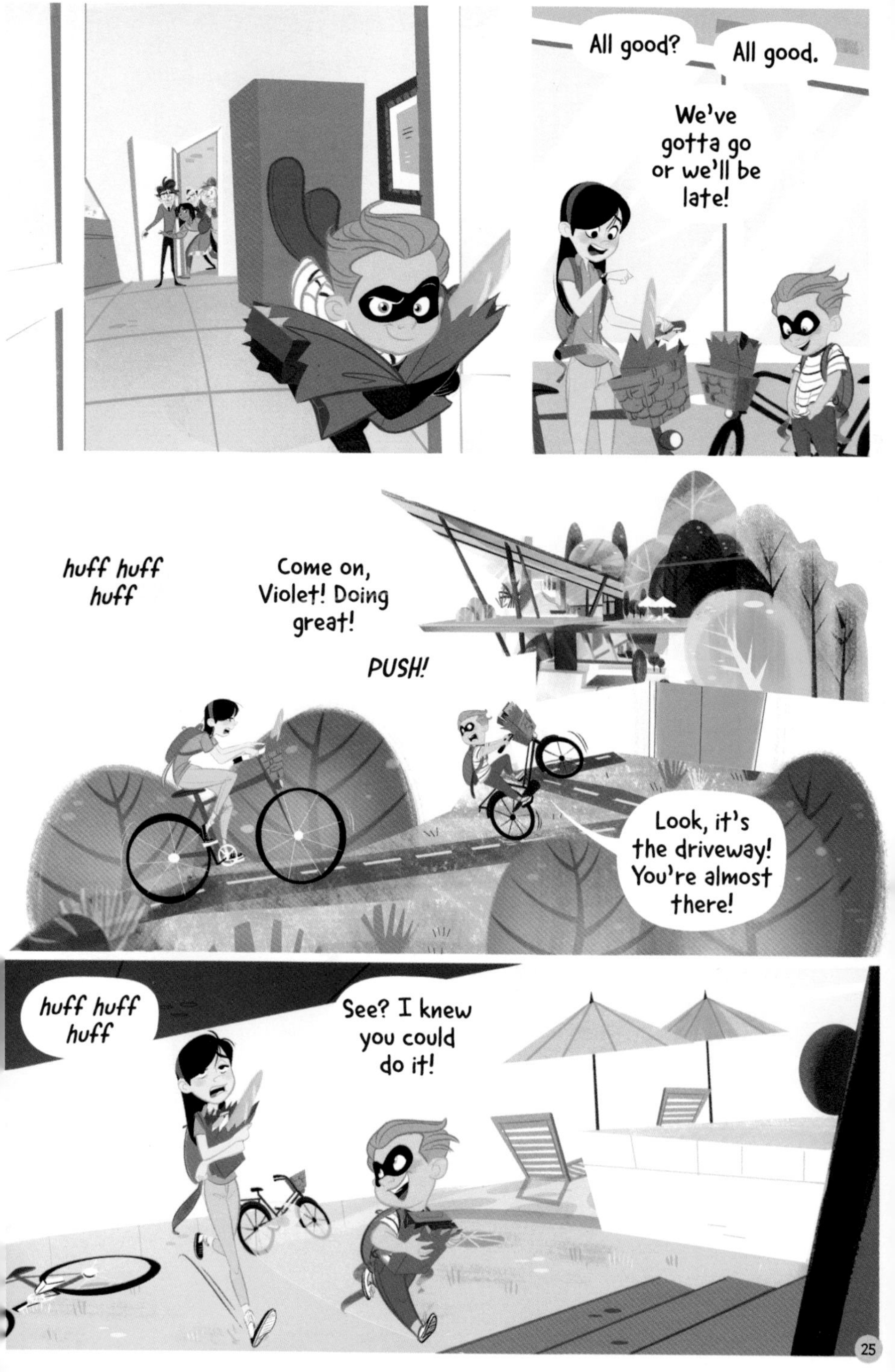
All good?
All good.
We've gotta go or we'll be late!
huff huff huff
Come on, Violet! Doing great!
PUSH!
Look, it's the driveway! You're almost there!
huff huff huff
See? I knew you could do it!

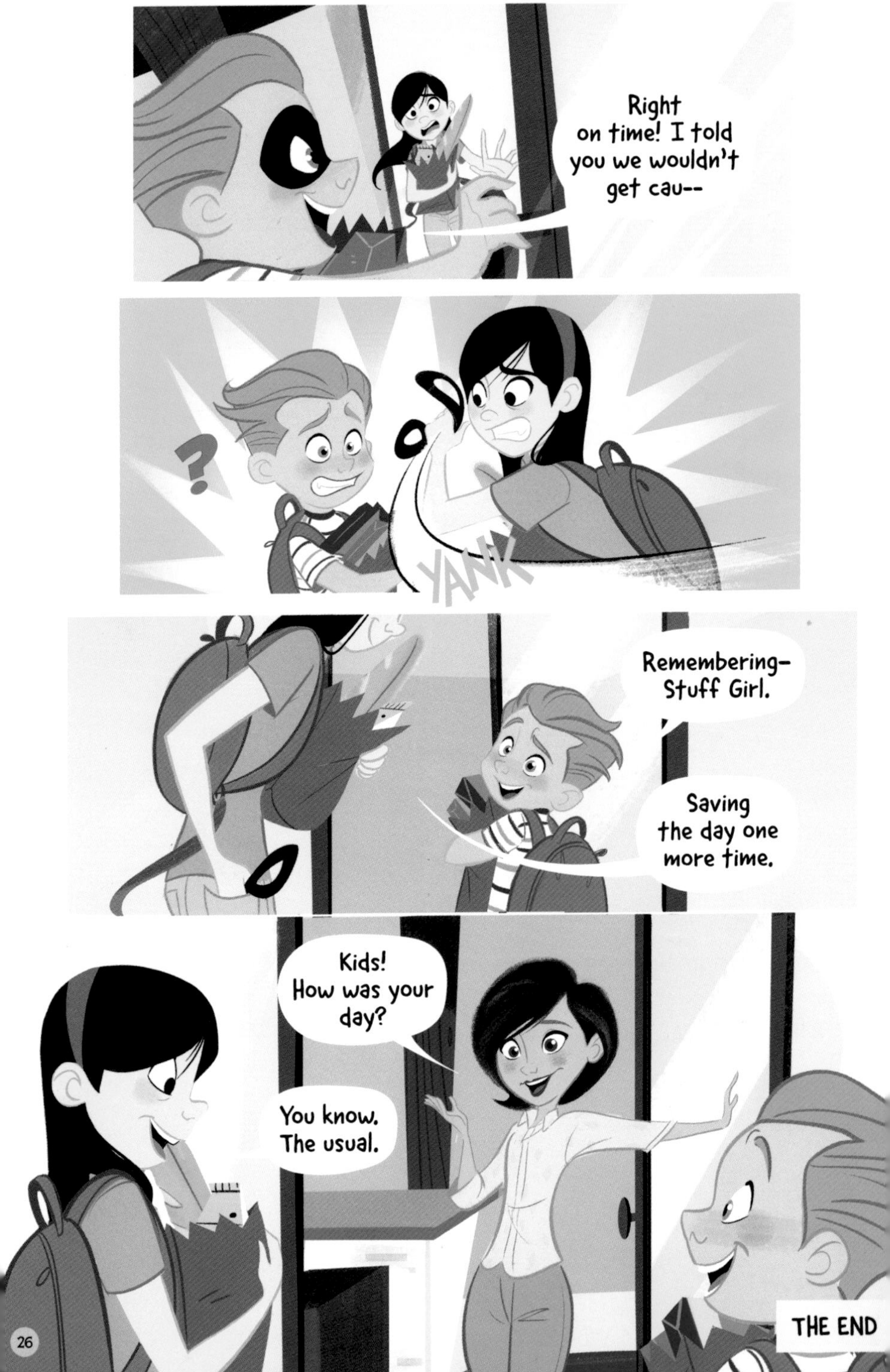
Right on time! I told you we wouldn't get cau--
?
YANK
Remembering-Stuff Girl.
Saving the day one more time.
Kids! How was your day?
You know. The usual.
THE END

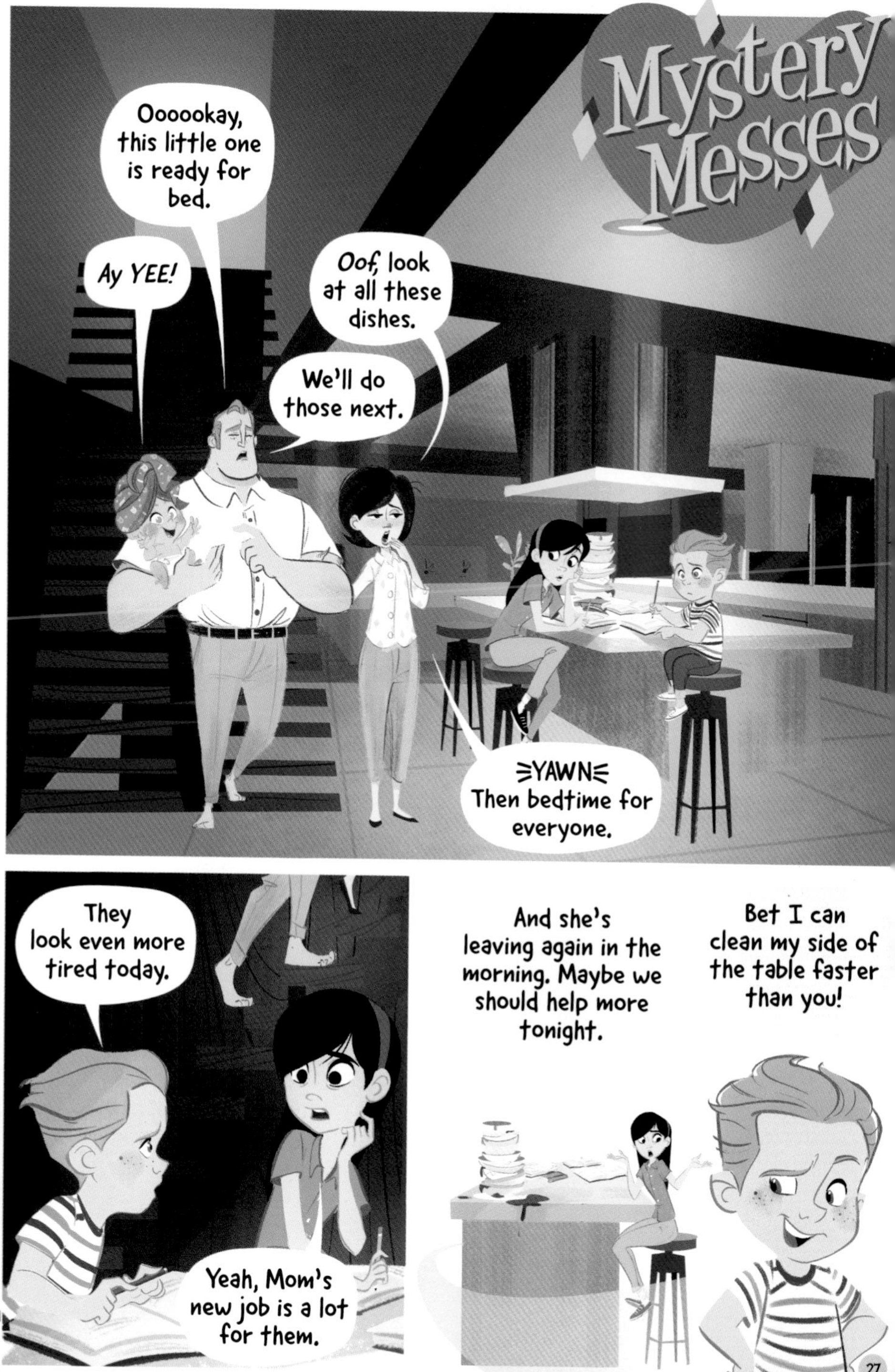
Mystery Messes
Oooookay, this little one is ready for bed.
Ay YEE!
Oof, look at all these dishes.
We'll do those next.
≡YAWN≡ Then bedtime for everyone.
They look even more tired today.
Yeah, Mom's new job is a lot for them.
And she's leaving again in the morning. Maybe we should help more tonight.
Bet I can clean my side of the table faster than you!

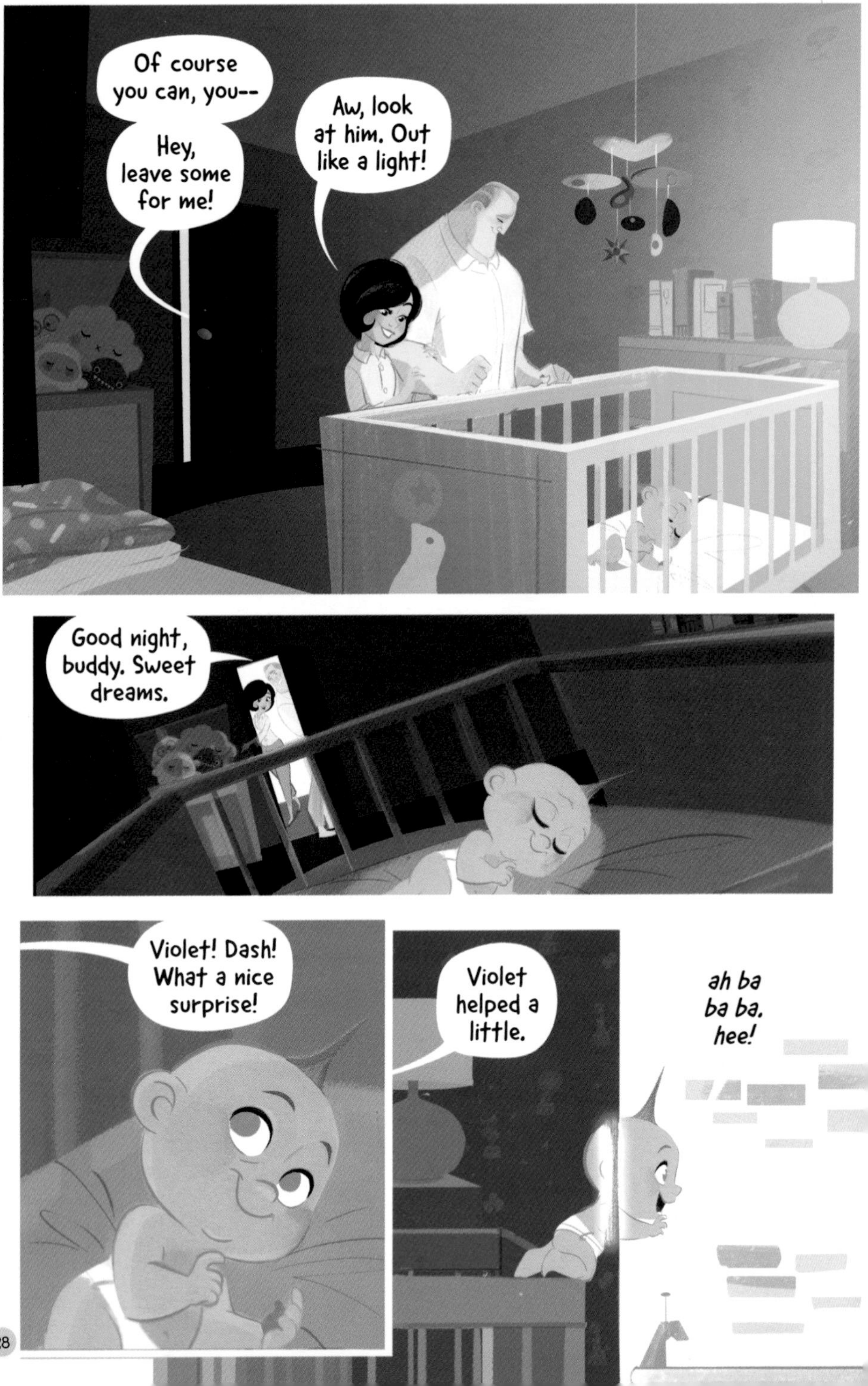
Of course you can, you--
Hey, leave some for me!
Aw, look at him. Out like a light!
Good night, buddy. Sweet dreams.
Violet! Dash! What a nice surprise!
Violet helped a little.
ah ba ba ba. hee!

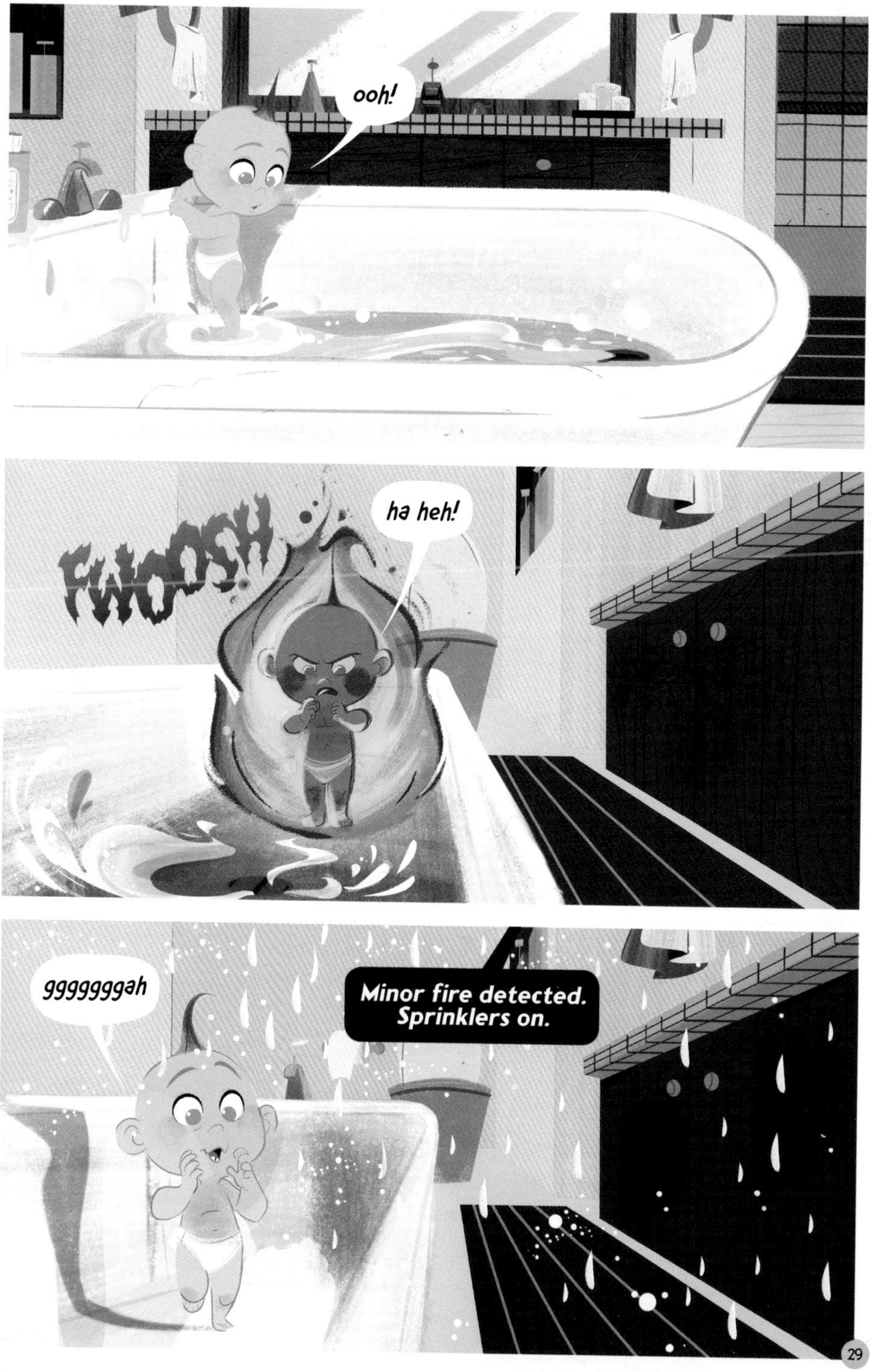
ooh!
FWOOSH
ha heh!
ggggggggah
Minor fire detected. Sprinklers on.

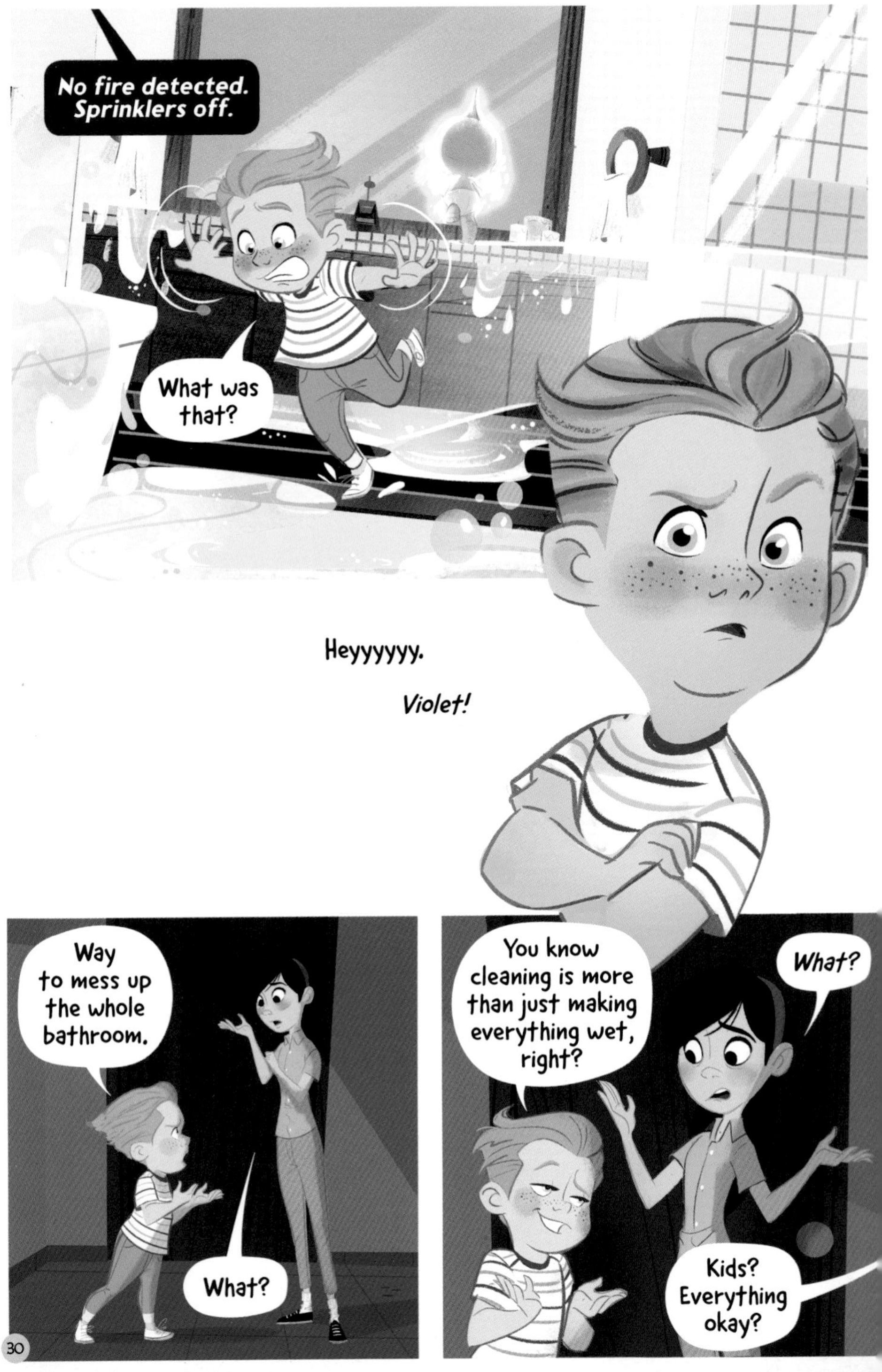
No fire detected. Sprinklers off.
What was that?
Heyyyyyy.
Violet!
Way to mess up the whole bathroom.
What?
You know cleaning is more than just making everything wet, right?
What?
Kids? Everything okay?

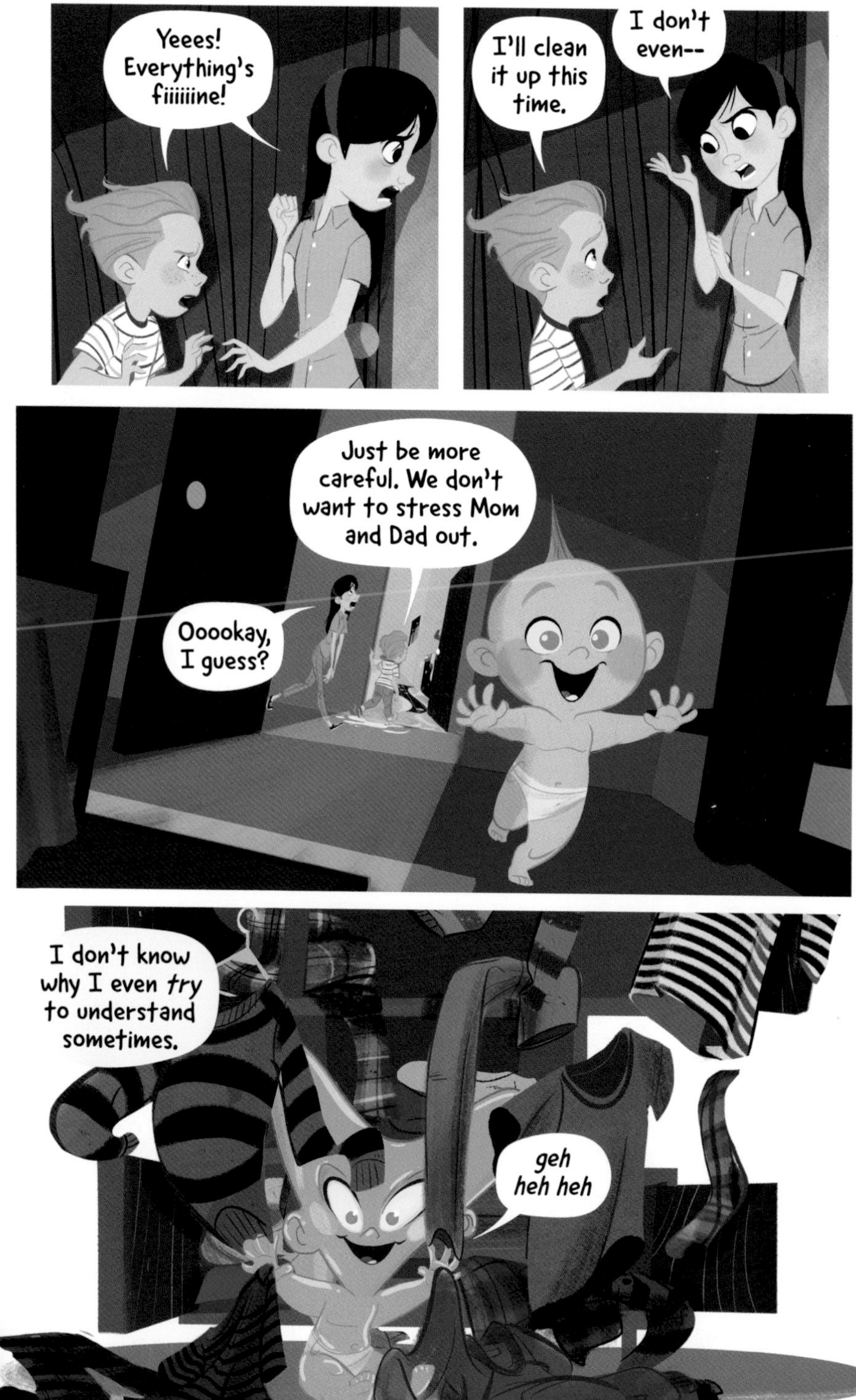
Yeees! Everything's fiiiiiine!
I'll clean it up this time.
I don't even--
Just be more careful. We don't want to stress Mom and Dad out.
Ooookay, I guess?
I don't know why I even *try* to understand sometimes.
geh heh heh

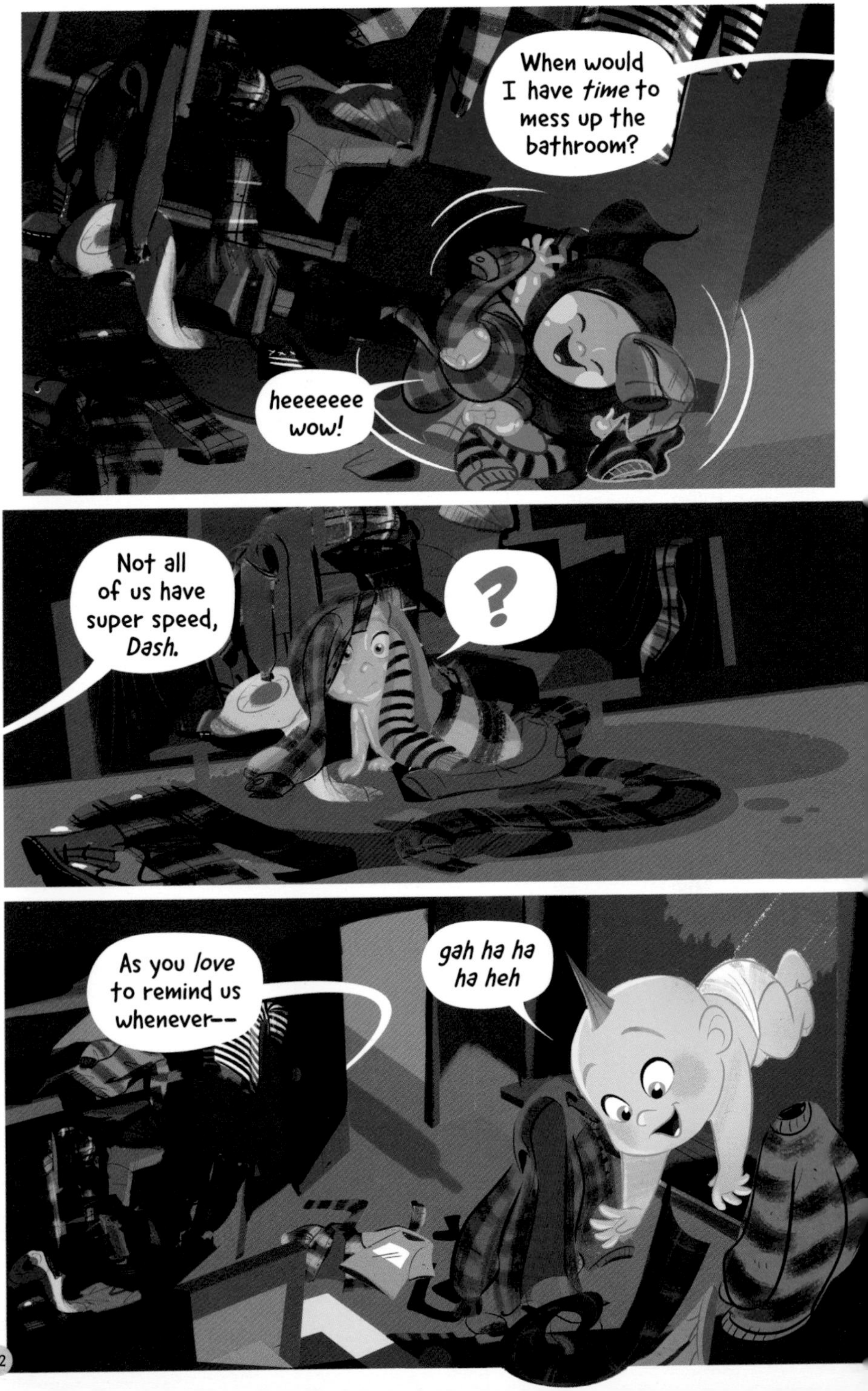
When would I have *time* to mess up the bathroom?
heeeeeee wow!
Not all of us have super speed, *Dash.*
?
As you *love* to remind us whenever--
gah ha ha ha heh

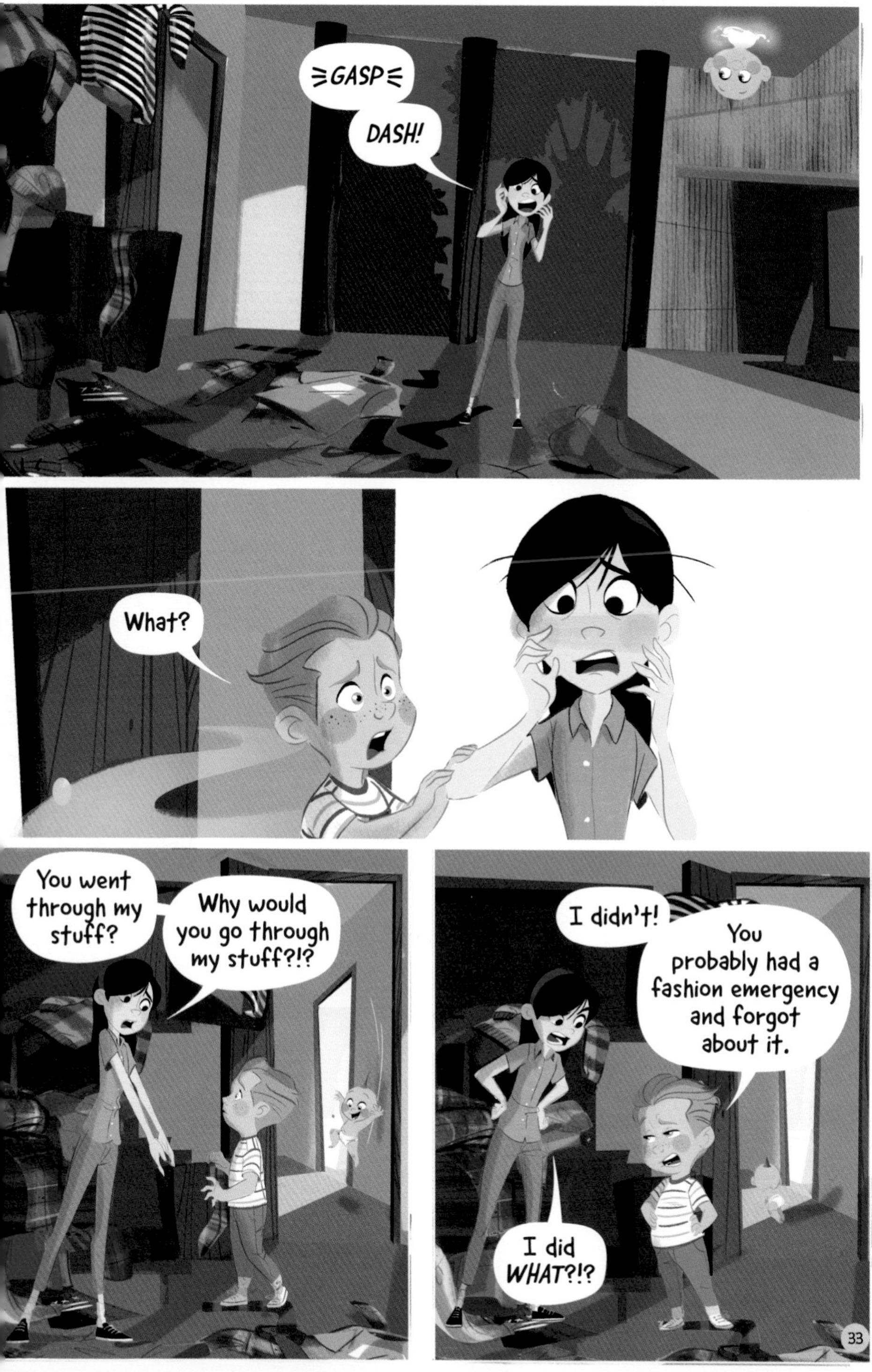

GASP
DASH!
What?
You went through my stuff?
Why would you go through my stuff?!?
I didn't!
You probably had a fashion emergency and forgot about it.
I did WHAT?!?

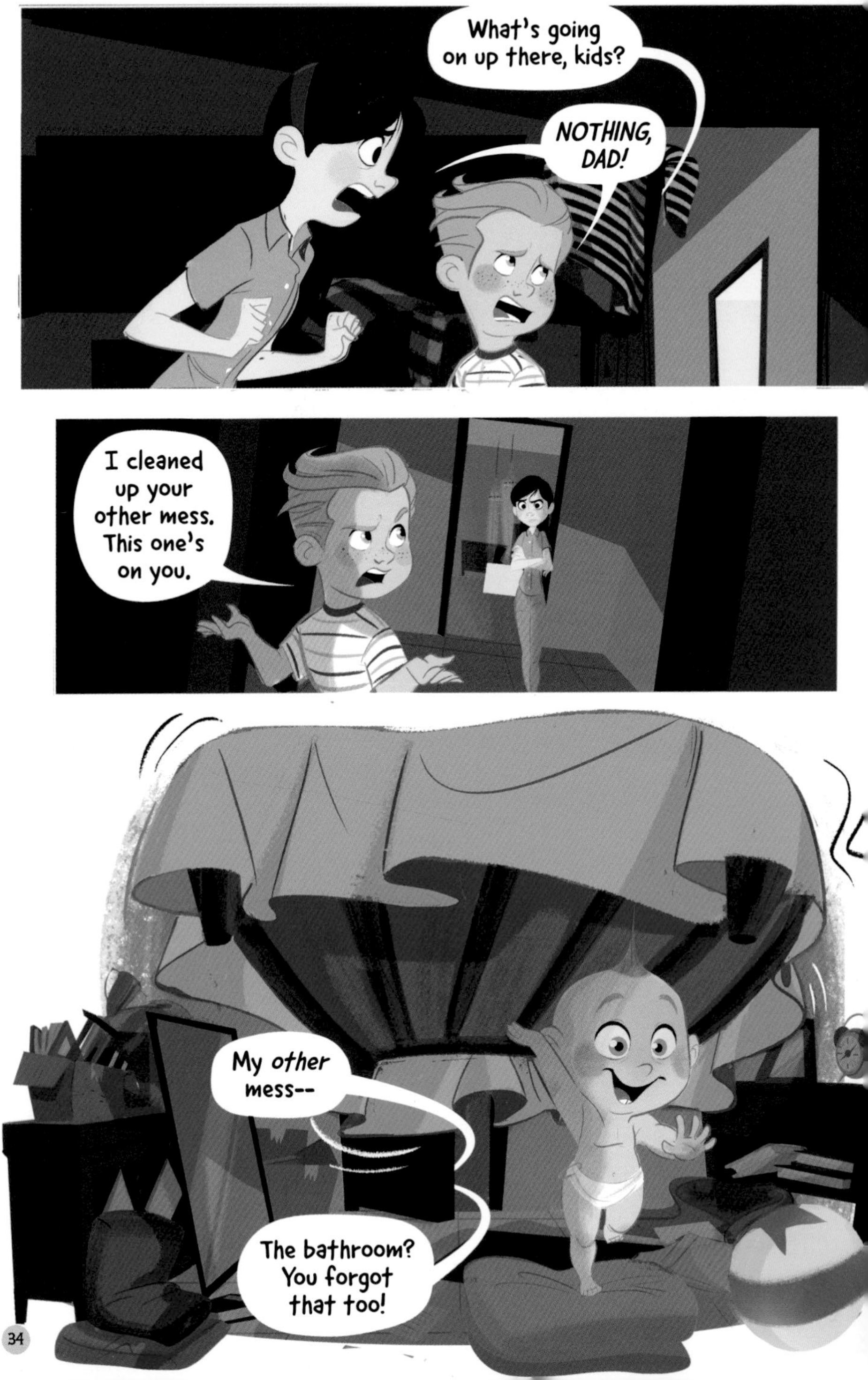
What's going on up there, kids?
NOTHING, DAD!
I cleaned up your other mess. This one's on you.
My *other* mess--
The bathroom? You forgot that too!

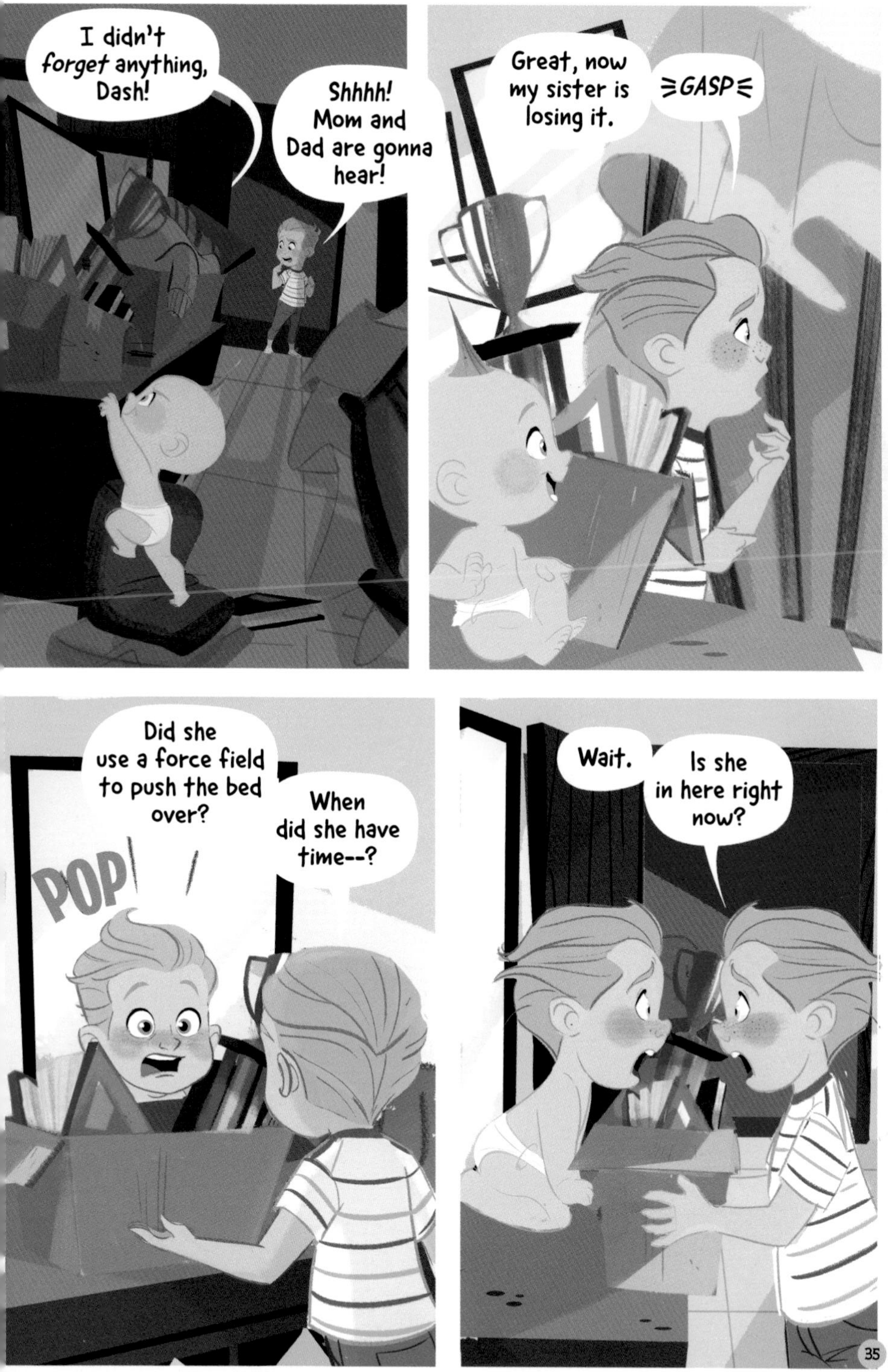
I didn't *forget* anything, Dash!
Shhhh! Mom and Dad are gonna hear!
Great, now my sister is losing it.
GASP
Did she use a force field to push the bed over?
When did she have time--?
POP
Wait.
Is she in here right now?

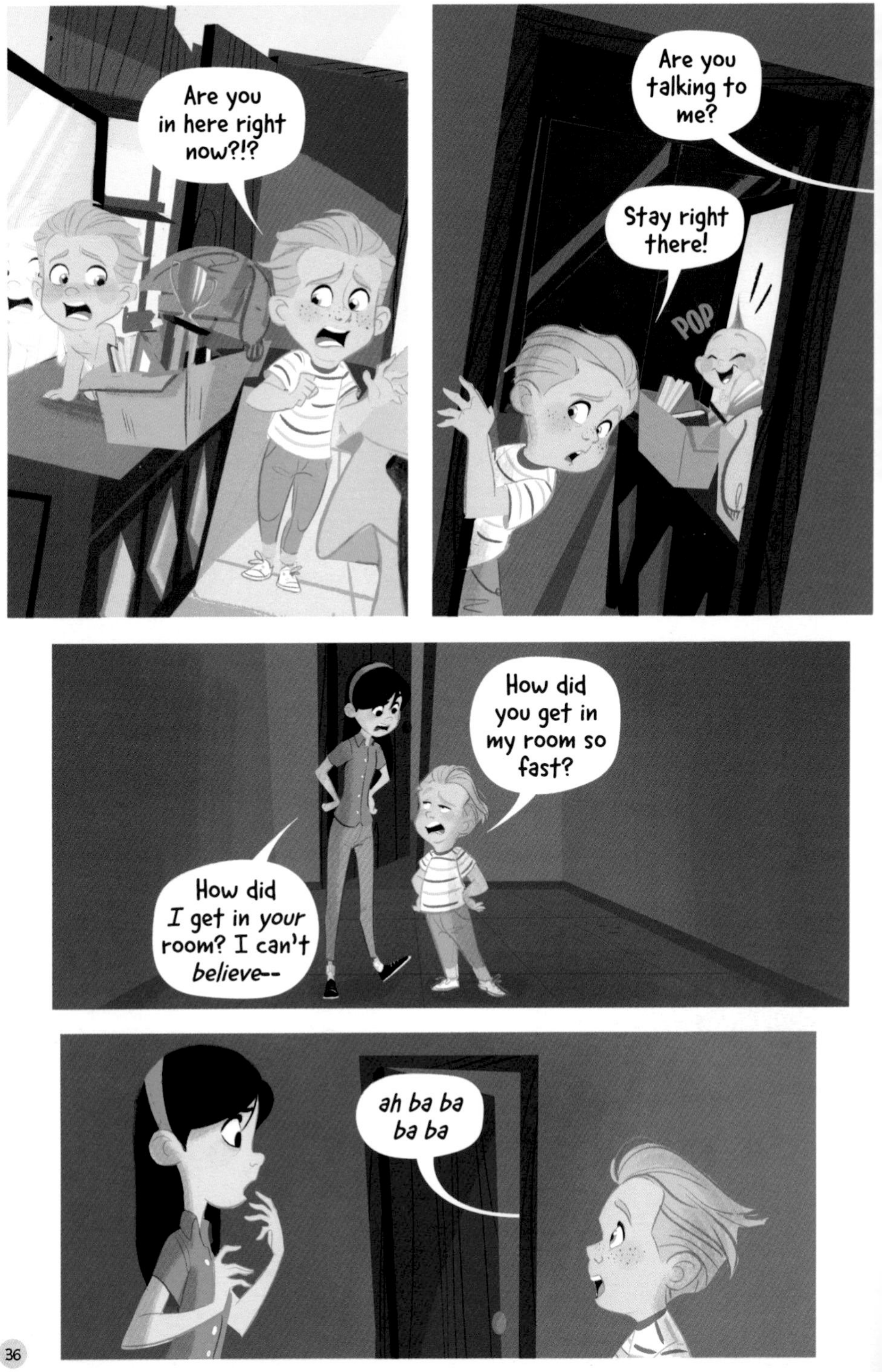
Are you in here right now?!?
Are you talking to me?
Stay right there!
POP
How did you get in my room so fast?
How did *I* get in *your* room? I can't *believe*--
ah ba ba ba ba

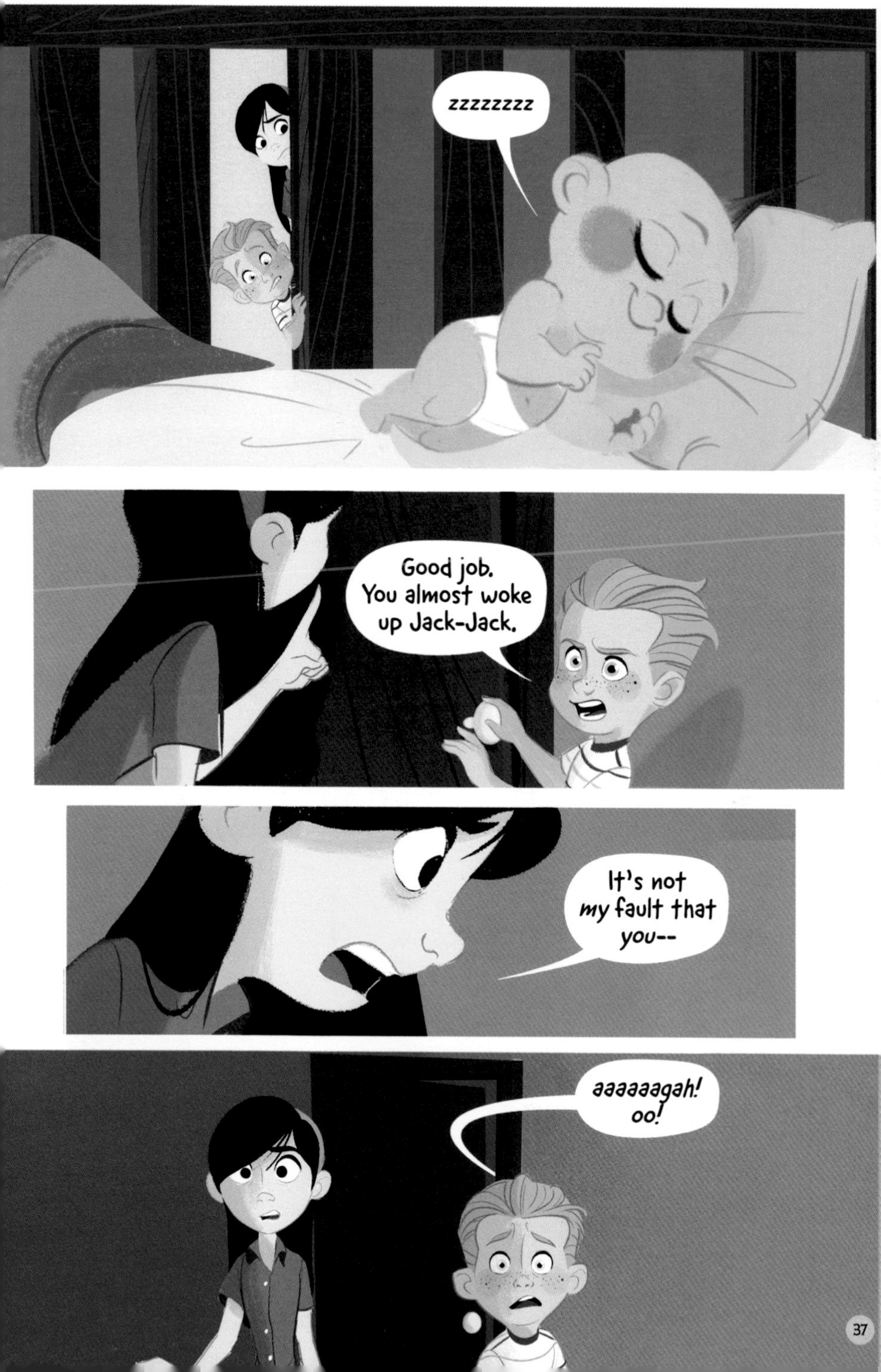
zzzzzzzz
Good job. You almost woke up Jack-Jack.
It's not my fault that you--
aaaaaagah! oo!

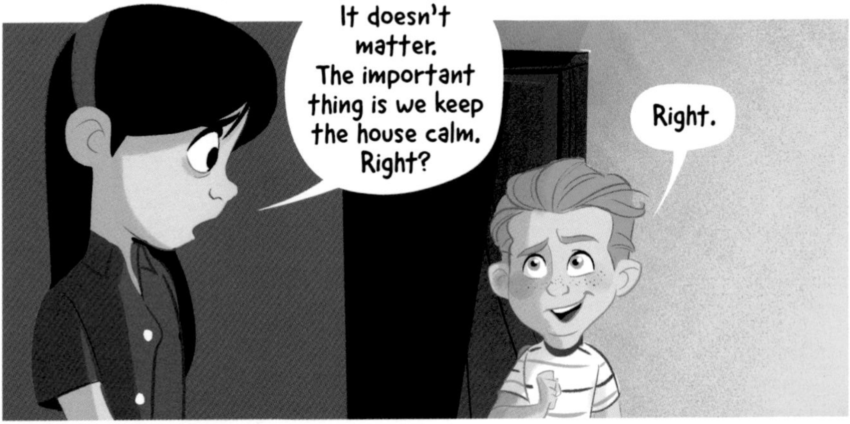
It doesn't matter. The important thing is we keep the house calm. Right?
Right.

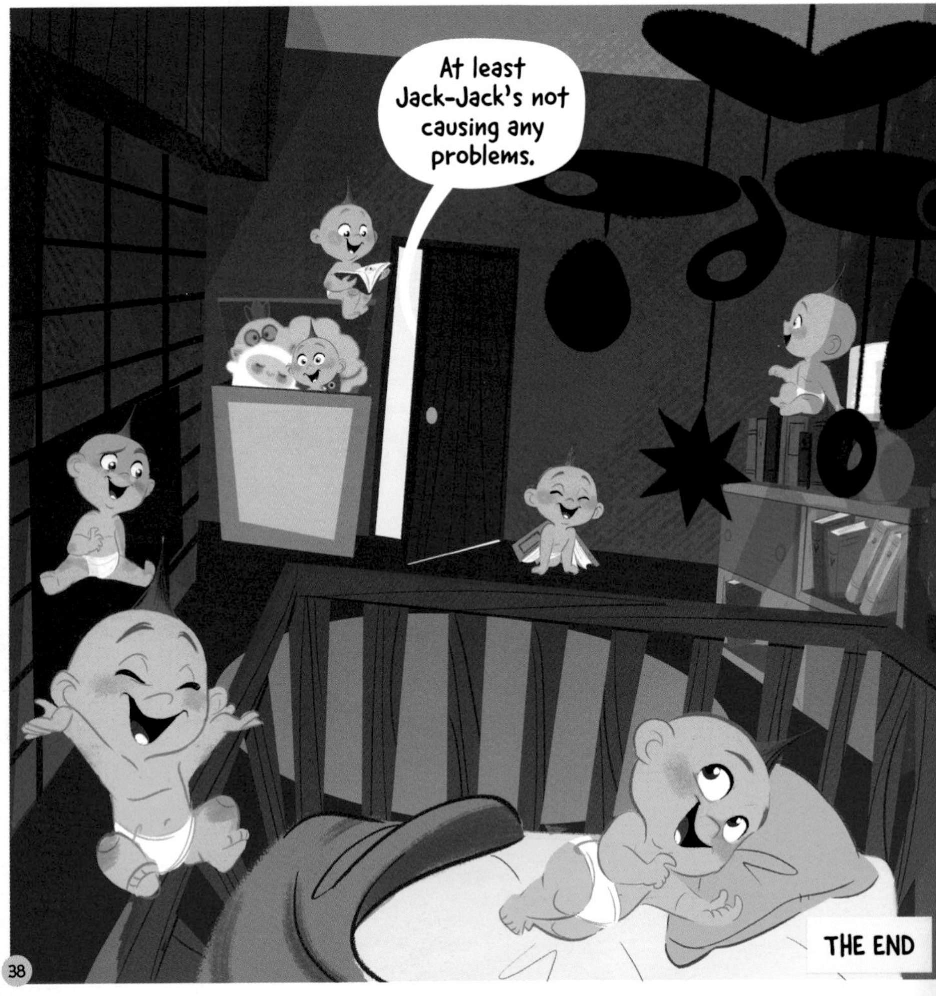
At least Jack-Jack's not causing any problems.
THE END

Activities and Extras for Incredible Fun!

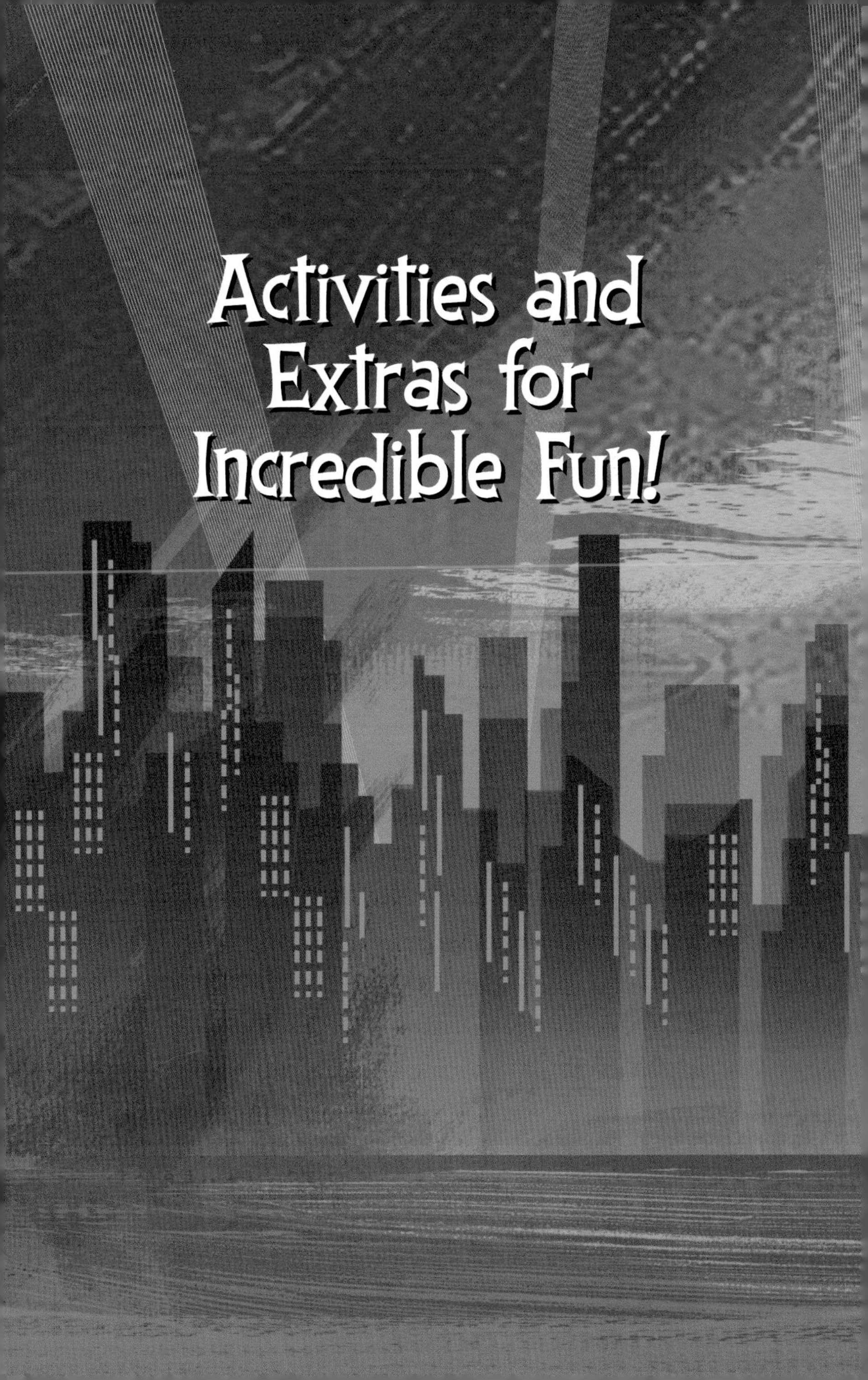

What's Missing

Look at the two pictures on these pages.
It's the same picture . . . or is it?
Can you spot 10 differences between picture A
and picture B? There are some things missing!

A

om the Picture?

When you think you've found all the differences,
you can check your answers at the bottom
of page 42!

B

Scavenger Hunt!

Can you find these items in the "SUPER-Market" story?

1 garbage can

2 dollars and cents

3 pick-axe

CHOCO
CEREAL

4 box of cereal

5 man with a dog

Can you find these items in the "Mystery Messes" story?

1 alarm clock

2 green lamp

3 stool

4 grey t-shirt

5 boot

What's Missing from the Picture answer key:

Scavenger Hunt answer key:

"SUPER-Market": garbage can, page 20; dollars and cents, page 24; pick-axe, page 10; box of cereal, page 18, 19, 26; man with a dog, page 23

"Mystery Messes": alarm clock, page 34; green lamp, page 28; stool, page 27; grey t-shirt, page 31; boot, page 32

How to Make a Comic!

Do you ever wonder how a comic is made? Over the next few pages, you can see the steps involved in creating one of the pages in this very book—from the beginning all the way to the finished product!

This is the script for page 6 of the "SUPER-Market" story.

As you can see, each panel description tells the artist exactly what to draw.

PAGE 6

PANEL 1
Invisible Violet sprints the few steps toward the hostages. She raises her hand to summon a shield. The hostages and the thief guarding them are flinching and covering their heads; no one is looking.

The script also includes the dialogue that the characters will be saying so that the artist can make sure to leave enough space for the balloons that will contain the dialogue.

EMPLOYEES (various):
Look out!
It's gonna hit us!
Noooo!

PANEL 2
Invisible Violet has thrown up a shield just in time to protect both her and the hostages, and the debris pings harmlessly off of it. Everyone except her still has their eyes covered.

SOUND EFFECTS (debris hitting shield, various sizes):
clunk
ping
WHACK
THUNK

PANEL 3
Hostage point of view now. They open their eyes and are astonished to see a perfect clear circle ringed by chunks of concrete and debris. Is it...a miracle?

AN EMPLOYEE
What...?

The dialogue can also help the artist decide how to draw the expressions and attitudes of the characters.

ANOTHER EMPLOYEE
Nothing hit us?

A THIRD EMPLOYEE
It's a miracle!

Special Tip! When you are writing a comic script and creating descriptions for each panel, try to visualize what you want to see in the panel—that will help you tell the artist exactly what they need to know!

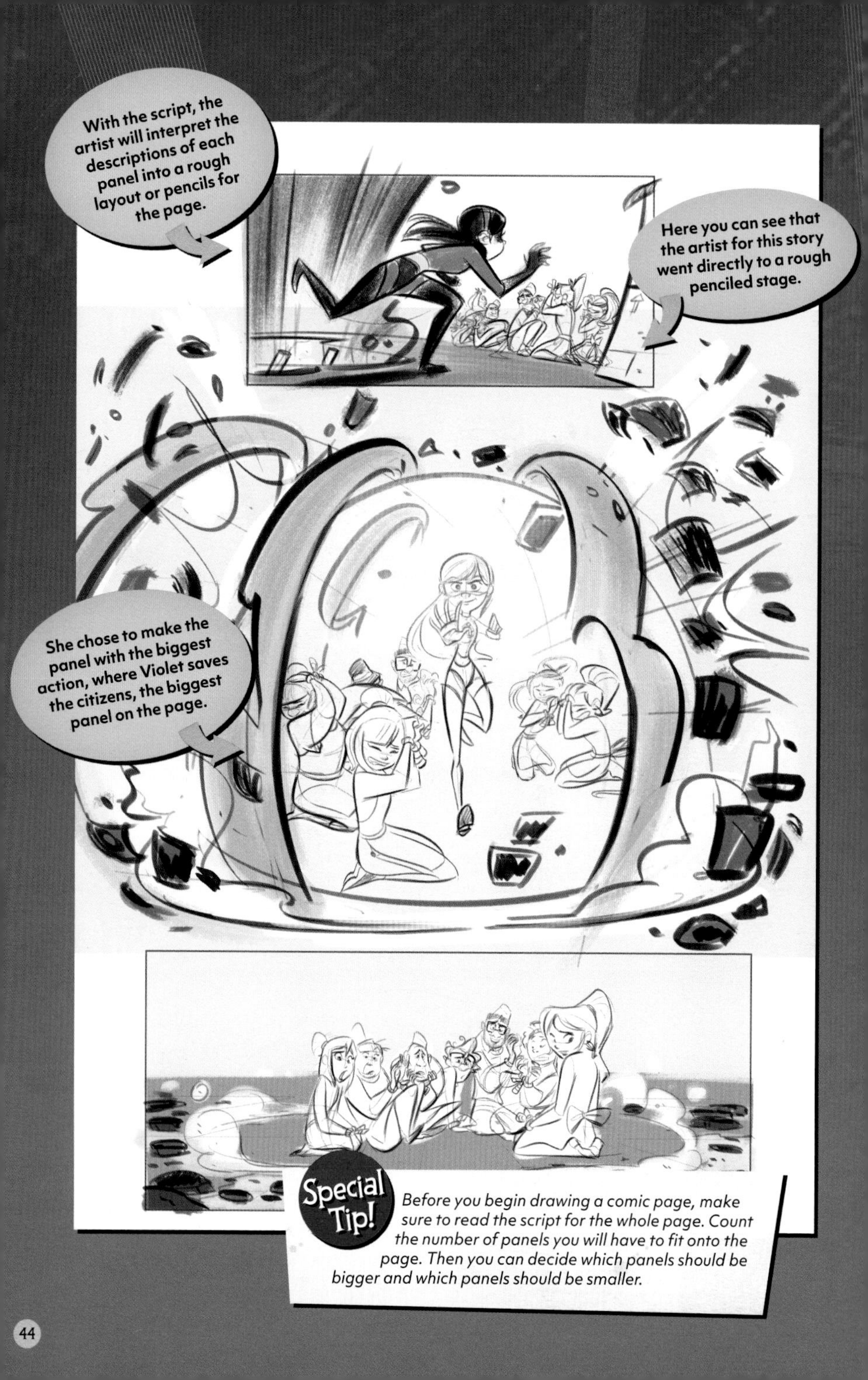

With the script, the artist will interpret the descriptions of each panel into a rough layout or pencils for the page.

Here you can see that the artist for this story went directly to a rough penciled stage.

She chose to make the panel with the biggest action, where Violet saves the citizens, the biggest panel on the page.

Special Tip! *Before you begin drawing a comic page, make sure to read the script for the whole page. Count the number of panels you will have to fit onto the page. Then you can decide which panels should be bigger and which panels should be smaller.*

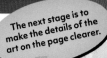

The next stage is to make the details of the art on the page clearer.

Depending on the artist that might be a stage called "tight pencils" or "inks."

But for this artist the next stage is "coloring" (or "painting") the page. Here you can see her final colored page.

Special Tip!

Think about what colors you want to use to help portray the different moods in your panels. Try using warm colors (yellow, orange, red) for action scenes, and cool colors (blue, purple, green) for calm scenes.

While the coloring is being created for a comic book page, the word balloons (also called "lettering") are also being created.

Look out!

It's gonna hit us!

Noooo!

With the script and the penciled page, a letterer will create balloons to contain each piece of dialogue, and place each balloon on the page.

THUNK

Finally, after lettering and colors are finished, they are put together to create the final page—which you can see here (and also on page 12 of this volume).

Nothing hit us?

What...?

It's a miracle!

Special Tip!

If you are drawing in your own word balloons by hand, something you can do to make sure that all the words fit inside the balloon is to write the words out on your page first, and then draw the balloon around them!

Do you make up stories sometimes? Next time you think of a story, you could make your own comic book! You could write your own script, draw all the panels, draw all the word balloons, and color it, too! And, if you used characters from the *Incredibles 2*, like Violet, Dash, and Jack-Jack, it would be a *Super* comic book story—just like the ones in this book! 😉

DARK HORSE BOOKS

president and publisher Mike Richardson • collection editor Freddye Miller •
collection assistant editors Jenny Blenk & Kevin Burkhalter • collection designer David Nestelle •
digital art technician Christianne Gillenardo-Goudreau

Neil Hankerson Executive Vice President • Tom Weddle Chief Financial Officer • Randy Stradley Vice
President of Publishing • Nick McWhorter Chief Business Development Officer • Matt Parkinson Vice
President of Marketing • Dale LaFountain Vice President of Information Technology • Cara Niece Vice
President of Production and Scheduling • Mark Bernardi Vice President of Book Trade and Digital Sales •
Ken Lizzi General Counsel • Dave Marshall Editor in Chief • Davey Estrada Editorial Director • Chris Warner
Senior Books Editor • Cary Grazzini Director of Specialty Projects • Lia Ribacchi Art Director • Vanessa
Todd-Holmes Director of Print Purchasing • Matt Dryer Director of Digital Art and Prepress • Michael
Gombos Director of International Publishing and Licensing • Kari Yadro Director of Custom Programs

DISNEY PUBLISHING WORLDWIDE GLOBAL MAGAZINES, COMICS AND PARTWORKS

Publisher Lynn Waggoner • EDITORIAL TEAM Bianca Coletti (Director, Magazines), Guido Frazzini
(Director, Comics), Carlotta Quattrocolo (Executive Editor), Stefano Ambrosio (Executive Editor, New IP),
Camilla Vedove (Senior Manager, Editorial Development), Behnoosh Khalili (Senior Editor), Julie Dorris
(Senior Editor), Mina Riazi (Assistant Editor), Jonathan Manning (Assistant Editor) • DESIGN Enrico Soave
(Senior Designer) • ART Ken Shue (VP, Global Art), Manny Mederos (Senior Illustration Manager, Comics
and Magazines), Roberto Santillo (Creative Director), Marco Ghiglione (Creative Manager), Stefano
Attardi (Computer Art Designer) • PORTFOLIO MANAGEMENT •Olivia Ciancarelli (Director) • BUSINESS
& MARKETING Mariantonietta Galla (Marketing Manager), Virpi Korhonen (Editorial Manager)

Incredibles 2: Heroes at Home

Published by Dark Horse Books
A division of Dark Horse Comics, Inc.
10956 SE Main Street
Milwaukie, OR 97222

DarkHorse.com

To find a comics shop in your area, visit comicshoplocator.com

First edition: June 2018
ISBN 978-1-50670-943-7

1 3 5 7 9 10 8 6 4 2
Printed in the United States of America

BOOKS THAT MIDDLE READERS WILL LOVE!

AVATAR: THE LAST AIRBENDER

Aang and friends' adventures continue right where the TV series left off, in these beautiful oversized hardcover collections, from *Airbender* creators Michael Dante DiMartino and Bryan Konietzko and Eisner and Harvey Award winner Gene Luen Yang!

The Promise ISBN 978-1-61655-074-5
The Search ISBN 978-1-61655-226-8
The Rift ISBN 978-1-61655-550-4
Smoke and Shadow ISBN 978-1-50670-013-7
North and South ISBN 978-1-50670-195-0
(Available October 2017)
$39.99 each

PLANTS VS. ZOMBIES

The hit video game continues its comic book invasion! Crazy Dave—the babbling-yet-brilliant inventor and top-notch neighborhood defender—helps his niece Patrice and young adventurer Nate Timely fend off a zombie invasion! Their only hope is a brave army of chomping, squashing, and pea-shooting plants!

Boxed Set #1: Lawnmageddon, Timepocalypse, Bully for You
ISBN 978-1-50670-043-4
Boxed Set #2: Grown Sweet Home, Garden Warfare, The Art of Plants vs. Zombies
ISBN 978-1-50670-232-2
Boxed Set #3: Petal to the Metal, Boom Boom Mushroom, Battle Extravagonzo
ISBN 978-1-50670-521-7 (Available October 2017)
$29.99 each

TREE MAIL
Mike Raicht, Brian Smith

Rudy—a determined frog—hopes to overcome the odds and land his dream job delivering mail to the other animals on Popomoko Island! Rudy always hops forward, no matter what obstacle seems to be in the way of his dreams!

ISBN 978-1-50670-096-0 **$12.99**

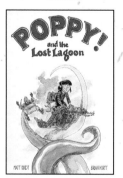

HOW TO TRAIN YOUR DRAGON: THE SERPENT'S HEIR

Picking up just after the events in *How to Train Your Dragon 2*, Hiccup, Astrid, and company are called upon to assist the people of an earthquake-plagued island. But their lives are imperiled by a madman and an incredible new dragon who even Toothless— the alpha dragon—may not be able to control!

ISBN 978-1-61655-931-1 **$10.99**

POPPY! AND THE LOST LAGOON
Matt Kindt, Brian Hurtt

At the age of ten, Poppy Pepperton is the greatest explorer since her grandfather Pappy! When a shrunken mummy head speaks, adventure calls Poppy and her sidekick/guardian, Colt Winchester, across the globe in search of an exotic fish—along the way discovering clues to what happened to Pappy all those years ago!

ISBN 978-1-61655-943-4 **$14.99**

SOUPY LEAVES HOME
Cecil Castellucci, Jose Pimienta

Two misfits with no place to call home take a train-hopping journey from the cold heartbreak of their eastern homes to the sunny promise of California in this Depression-era coming-of-age tale.

ISBN 978-1-61655-431-6 **$14.99**

DARKHORSE.COM
AVAILABLE AT YOUR LOCAL COMICS SHOP OR BOOKSTORE | TO FIND A COMICS SHOP IN YOUR AREA, CALL 1-888-266-4226
For more information or to order direct: On the web: DarkHorse.com •Email: mailorder@darkhorse.com •Phone: 1-800-862-0052 Mon.–Fri. 9 AM to 5 PM Pacific Time.
Avatar: The Last Airbender © Viacom International Inc. Plants vs. Zombies © Electronic Arts Inc. How to Train Your Dragon © DreamWorks Animation LLC. Tree Mail™ © Brian Smith and Noble Transmission Group, LLC.
Poppy!™ © Matt Kindt and Brian Hurtt. Soupy Leaves Home™ © Cecil Castellucci. Dark Horse Books® and the Dark Horse logo are registered trademarks of Dark Horse Comics, Inc. All rights reserved. (BL 6002 PI)